The Club of
Queer Trades

The Club of Queer Trades

G.K. Chesterton

ET REMOTISSIMA PROPE

Modern Voices

Modern Voices
Published by Hesperus Press Limited
4 Rickett Street, London SW6 1RU
www.hesperuspress.com

The Club of Queer Trades first published in 1905
A Defence of Detective Stories first published in *The Speaker* in 1901
First published by Hesperus Press Limited, 2007

Foreword © Gilbert Adair, 2007

Designed and typeset by Fraser Muggeridge studio
Printed in Jordan by the Jordan National Press

ISBN: 1-84391-434-4
ISBN13: 978-1-84391-434-1

Contents

Foreword

There was never just one G.K. Chesterton. There was Chesterton the Catholic proselytiser, the hearty balladeer of Merrie England, the harrumphing castigator of teetotallers and vegetarians, the blustery anti-Communist, anti-plutocrat and also, alas, anti-Semite. There was Chesterton the charmer of children – one little boy, asked after a visit to the great man's home if G.K.C. had been awfully clever, replied, 'I don't know about clever, but you should see him catch buns in his mouf.' There was Chesterton the week-in-week-out jobbing journalist, producing essays on every subject under the sun, whether it be the intellectual inferiority of MPs to the populace they are elected to serve ('the blind leading the people who can see') or what he regarded as the inherent contrariness of feminism ('women asserted that they would not be dictated to, but then became stenographers'). There was Chesterton the polemicist, eternally twinned, like a pantomime horse, with his close friend and sparring partner, Hilaire Belloc. There was Chesterton the aphorist and Chesterton the metaphorist. There was the Chesterton who employed paradoxes (the feeblest of which were little more than platitudes performing handstands, while the best were as brilliant as Wilde's) with the relish and frequency that contemporary writers employ swear words. And there was, supremely, the Chesterton who concerns us here, the only one of the litter to have survived (nine-tenths of his writings are currently out of print): Chesterton the deviser of the craftiest detective stories in the English language.

The most popular of his stories, of course, remain those featuring Father Brown, but Chesterton had lots of others published, either in magazines or between hard covers. He wasn't one of those writers constrained by material imperatives to expend his quotidian energy on what he secretly repudiated as hack work, while dreaming of the masterpieces he would create if only he had the time. He took the detective story seriously enough to write a sprightly defence of the genre (published in this volume) and was, alongside Agatha Christie, Dorothy Sayers, Anthony Berkeley et al, an assiduous member of the Detection Club. It's hard to believe he would have been aghast to discover that, if his name is still a conjurable one, it's almost exclusively because of his mystery fiction.

The six episodes of *The Club of Queer Trades* (a title that, in this less innocent century of ours, would carry a rather raunchily ambiguous connotation) are not, *senso stricto*, detective stories at all, and they are certainly not mini-whodunits: what interested Chesterton was not the least likely suspect but the least likely motive. Their basic structure, however, is exactly comparable to those of the Father Brown adventures. An impossible effect is described, only to be shown, with a climactic flourish, to have had a perfectly possible cause all along. In the fourth story, 'The Singular Speculation of the House-Agent', Chesterton's protagonist and alter ego (or alter egoist), Basil Grant, a whimsical judge-turned-*flâneur*, remarks, 'Truth must of necessity be stranger than fiction, for fiction is the creation of the human mind, and therefore is congenial to it.' If, as one assumes, it is Chesterton himself who is speaking through Grant, then it was patently his ambition, in all of his shorter texts, to write fiction that would turn out to be stranger than truth.

Chesterton sought always to entertain – he was a reader's writer rather than a writer's writer. Yet even these light-textured tales (the members of the titular club must each practise a heretofore unheard-of profession) have, as is often the case with this author, a profoundly unsettling undertow. The Argentinian fabulist Jorge Luis Borges, a great admirer, once made an intriguing claim. He said that, while Dickens' fiction piled on the agonies of poverty, neglect, violence, solitude and death, the warmth of his style guaranteed that the society he depicted never ceased to be convivial. The ostensibly breezy, life-loving Chesterton, by contrast, tended to write nightmarish fictions full of ominously lurid sunsets and wild-eyed, red-haired young poets. Red hair, in fact, might be what semiologists term the trivial signifier of his entire imaginative world. Amazingly, no fewer than three of the characters in *The Club of Queer Trades* are red-haired, in just six stories, and on each occasion, given the eerie atmospherics, one cannot resist visualising that hair as literally red, practically blood-red.

Even if, in Chesterton's work, crimes that seem to be rooted in the pagan and the supernatural are invariably revealed, come the dénouement, to have had a reassuringly rational basis, an aftertaste of occult perversity lingers on, as it does from a proper nightmare. In short, the more one reads him, the more one begins to wonder whether this jolly, God-fearing man might just have been, in today's vulgar parlance, *sick*. It is, at any rate, his flesh-creeping proximity to Poe and Kafka and indeed Borges that makes him not just still readable but still modern.

Consider this passage from 'The Eccentric Seclusion of the Old Lady':

> We were walking along a lonely terrace in Brompton together. The street was full of that bright blue twilight which comes about half-past eight in summer, and which seems for the moment to be not so much a coming of darkness as the turning on of a new azure illuminator, as if the earth were lit suddenly by a sapphire sun. In the cool blue the lemon tint of the lamps had already begun to flame.

A sapphire sun! And not in Benares, mind you, but in Brompton! Chesterton was incapable of writing about humdrum old London without exoticising it and, though he may well never even have heard of Magritte, it is of Magritte's topsy-turvy nightscapes that one thinks when reading passages such as these (of which there are many in his work). Thus, congenitally hostile to all isms as he was, save of course Catholicism, he himself proved to be something of a Surrealist *avant la lettre*. And that, perhaps, was the crowning paradox of G.K. Chesterton.

– Gilbert Adair, 2007

The Club of
Queer Trades

The Tremendous Adventures of Major Brown

Rabelais, or his wild illustrator Gustave Doré,[1] must have had something to do with the designing of the things called flats in England and America. There is something entirely Gargantuan in the idea of economising space by piling houses on top of each other, front doors and all. And in the chaos and complexity of those perpendicular streets anything may dwell or happen, and it is in one of them, I believe, that the enquirer may find the offices of the Club of Queer Trades. It may be thought at the first glance that the name would attract and startle the passer-by, but nothing attracts or startles in these dim immense hives. The passer-by is only looking for his own melancholy destination, the Montenegro Shipping Agency or the London office of the *Rutland Sentinel*, and passes through the twilight passages as one passes through the twilight corridors of a dream. If the Thugs set up a Strangers' Assassination Company in one of the great buildings in Norfolk Street, and sent in a mild man in spectacles to answer enquiries, no enquiries would be made. And the Club of Queer Trades reigns in a great edifice hidden like a fossil in a mighty cliff of fossils.

The nature of this society, such as we afterwards discovered it to be, is soon and simply told. It is an eccentric and Bohemian club, of which the absolute condition of membership lies in this, that the candidate must have invented the method by which he earns his living. It must be an entirely new trade. The exact definition of this requirement is given in the two principal rules. First, it must not be a mere application or variation of an existing trade. Thus, for instance, the club would not admit an insurance agent simply because instead of insuring men's furniture against being burnt in a fire, he insured, let us say, their trousers against being torn by a mad dog. The principle (as Sir Bradcock Burnaby-Bradcock, in the extraordinarily eloquent and soaring speech to the club on the occasion of the question being raised in the Stormby Smith affair, said wittily and keenly) is the same. Secondly, the trade must be a genuine commercial source of income, the support of its inventor. Thus the club would not receive a man simply because he chose to pass his days collecting broken sardine tins, unless he could drive a roaring trade in them. Professor Chick made that quite clear. And when one remembers what Professor Chick's own new trade was, one doesn't know whether to laugh or cry.

The discovery of this strange society was a curiously refreshing thing; to realise that there were ten new trades in the world was like looking at the first ship or the first plough. It made a man feel what he should feel, that he was still in the childhood of the world. That I should have come at last upon so singular a body was, I may say without vanity, not altogether singular, for I have a mania for belonging to as many societies as possible: I may be said to collect clubs, and I have accumulated a vast and fantastic variety of specimens ever since, in my audacious youth, I collected the Athenaeum.[2] At some future day, perhaps, I may tell tales of some of the other bodies to which I have belonged. I will recount the doings of the Dead Man's Shoes Society (that superficially immoral, but darkly justifiable communion); I will explain the curious origin of the Cat and Christian, the name of which has been so shamefully misinterpreted; and the world shall know at last why the Institute of Typewriters coalesced with the Red Tulip League. Of the Ten Teacups, of course I dare not say a word. The first of my revelations, at any rate, shall be concerned with the Club of Queer Trades, which, as I have said, was one of this class, one that I was almost bound to come across sooner or later, because of my singular hobby. The wild youth of the

4

metropolis call me facetiously 'The King of Clubs'. They also call me 'The Cherub', in allusion to the roseate and youthful appearance I have presented in my declining years. I only hope the spirits in the better world have as good dinners as I have. But the finding of the Club of Queer Trades has one very curious thing about it. The most curious thing about it is that it was not discovered by me; it was discovered by my friend Basil Grant, a star-gazer, a mystic and a man who scarcely stirred out of his attic.

Very few people knew anything of Basil; not because he was in the least unsociable, for if a man out of the street had walked into his rooms he would have kept him talking till morning. Few people knew him, because, like all poets, he could do without them; he welcomed a human face as he might welcome a sudden blend of colour in a sunset; but he no more felt the need of going out to parties than he felt the need of altering the sunset clouds. He lived in a queer and comfortable garret in the roofs of Lambeth. He was surrounded by a chaos of things that were in odd contrast to the slums around him; old fantastic books, swords, armour – the whole dust hole of romanticism. But his face, amid all these quixotic relics, appeared curiously keen and modern – a powerful, legal face. And no one but I knew who he was.

Long ago as it is, everyone remembers the terrible and grotesque scene that occurred in —, when one of the most acute and forcible of the English judges suddenly went mad on the bench. I had my own view of that occurrence; but about the facts themselves there is no question at all. For some months, indeed for some years, people had detected something curious in the judge's conduct. He seemed to have lost interest in the law, in which he had been beyond expression brilliant and terrible as a KC,[3] and to be occupied in giving personal and moral advice to the people concerned. He talked more like a priest or a doctor, and a very outspoken one at that. The first thrill was probably given when he said to a man who had attempted a crime of passion: 'I sentence you to three years' imprisonment, under the firm, and solemn, and God-given conviction, that what you require is three months at the seaside.' He accused criminals from the bench, not so much of their obvious legal crimes, but of things that had never been heard of in a court of justice, monstrous egoism, lack of humour and morbidity deliberately encouraged. Things came to a head in that celebrated diamond case in which the Prime Minister himself, that brilliant patrician, had to come forward, gracefully and reluctantly, to give evidence against his valet. After the detailed life of the household had been thoroughly exhibited, the judge requested the Premier again to step forward, which he did with quiet dignity. The judge then said, in a sudden, grating voice: 'Get a new soul. That thing's not fit for a dog. Get a new soul.' All this, of course, in the eyes of the sagacious, was premonitory of that melancholy and farcical day when his wits actually deserted him in open court. It was a libel case between two very eminent and powerful financiers, against both of whom charges of considerable defalcation were brought. The case was long and complex; the advocates were long and eloquent; but at last, after weeks of work and rhetoric, the time came for the great judge to give a summing-up; and one of his celebrated masterpieces of lucidity and pulverising logic was eagerly looked for. He had spoken very little during the prolonged affair, and he looked sad and lowering at the end of it. He was silent for a few moments, and then burst into a stentorian song. His remarks (as reported) were as follows:

'O Rowty-owty tiddly-owty Tiddly-owty tiddly-owty Highty-ighty tiddly-ighty Tiddly-ighty ow.'

He then retired from public life and took the garret in Lambeth.

I was sitting there one evening, about six o'clock, over a glass of that gorgeous Burgundy which he kept behind a pile of black-letter folios; he was striding about the room, fingering, after a habit of his, one of the great swords in his collection; the red glare of the strong fire struck his square features and his fierce grey hair; his blue eyes were even unusually full of dreams, and he had opened his mouth to speak dreamily, when the door was flung open, and a pale, fiery man, with red hair and a huge furred overcoat, swung himself panting into the room.

'Sorry to bother you, Basil,' he gasped. 'I took a liberty – made an appointment here with a man – a client – in five minutes – I beg your pardon, sir,' and he gave me a bow of apology.

Basil smiled at me. 'You didn't know,' he said, 'that I had a practical brother. This is Rupert Grant, Esquire, who can and does all there is to be done. Just as I was a failure at one thing, he is a success at everything. I remember him as a journalist, a house-agent, a naturalist, an inventor, a publisher, a school-master, a – what are you now, Rupert?'

'I am and have been for some time,' said Rupert, with some dignity, 'a private detective, and there's my client.'

A loud rap at the door had cut him short, and, on permission being given, the door was thrown sharply open and a stout, dapper man walked swiftly into the room, set his silk hat with a clap on the table, and said, 'Good evening, gentlemen,' with a stress on the last syllable which somehow marked him out as a martinet, military, literary and social. He had a large head streaked with black and grey, and an abrupt black moustache, which gave him a look of fierceness which was contradicted by his sad sea-blue eyes.

Basil immediately said to me, 'Let us come into the next room, Gully,' and was moving towards the door, but the stranger said:

'Not at all. Friends remain. Assistance possibly.'

The moment I heard him speak I remembered who he was, a certain Major Brown I had met years before in Basil's society. I had forgotten altogether the black dandified figure and the large solemn head, but I remembered the peculiar speech, which consisted of only saying about a quarter of each sentence, and that sharply, like the crack of a gun. I do not know, it may have come from giving orders to troops.

Major Brown was a VC,[4] and an able and distinguished soldier, but he was anything but a warlike person. Like many among the iron men who recovered British India, he was a man with the natural beliefs and tastes of an old maid. In his dress he was dapper and yet demure; in his habits he was precise to the point of the exact adjustment of a teacup. One enthusiasm he had, which was of the nature of a religion – the cultivation of pansies. And when he talked about his collection, his blue eyes glittered like a child's at a new toy, the eyes that had remained untroubled when the troops were roaring victory round Roberts at Candahar.[5]

'Well, Major,' said Rupert Grant, with a lordly heartiness, flinging himself into a chair, 'what is the matter with you?'

'Yellow pansies. Coal-cellar. P.G. Northover,' said the Major, with righteous indignation.

We glanced at each other with inquisitiveness. Basil, who had his eyes shut in his abstracted way, said simply:

'I beg your pardon.'

'Fact is. Street, you know, man, pansies. On wall. Death to me. Something. Preposterous.'

We shook our heads gently. Bit by bit, and mainly by the seemingly sleepy assistance of Basil Grant, we pieced together the Major's fragmentary, but excited narration. It would be infamous to submit the reader to what we endured; therefore I will tell the story of Major Brown in my own words. But the reader must imagine the scene. The eyes of Basil closed as in a trance, after his habit, and the eyes of Rupert and myself getting rounder and rounder as we listened to one of the most astounding stories in the world, from the lips of the little man in black, sitting bolt upright in his chair and talking like a telegram.

Major Brown was, I have said, a successful soldier, but by no means an enthusiastic one. So far from regretting his retirement on half pay, it was with delight that he took a small neat villa, very like a doll's house, and devoted the rest of his life to pansies and weak tea. The thought that battles were over when he had once hung up his sword in the little front hall (along with two patent stewpots and a bad watercolour), and betaken himself instead to wielding the rake in his little sunlit garden, was to him like having come into a harbour in heaven. He was Dutchlike and precise in his taste in gardening, and had, perhaps, some tendency to drill his flowers like soldiers. He was one of those men who are capable of putting four umbrellas in the stand rather than three, so that two may lean one way and two another; he saw life like a pattern in a freehand drawing-book. And assuredly he would not have believed, or even understood, anyone who had told him that within a few yards of his brick paradise he was destined to be caught in a whirlpool of incredible adventure, such as he had never seen or dreamed of in the horrible jungle, or the heat of battle.

One certain bright and windy afternoon, the Major, attired in his usual faultless manner, had set out for his usual constitutional. In crossing from one great residential thoroughfare to another, he happened to pass along one of those aimless-looking lanes which lie along the back-garden walls of a row of mansions, and which in their empty and discoloured appearance give one an odd sensation as of being behind the scenes of a theatre. But mean and sulky as the scene might be in the eyes of most of us, it was not altogether so in the Major's, for along the coarse gravel footway was coming a thing which was to him what the passing of a religious procession is to a devout person. A large, heavy man, with fish-blue eyes and a ring of irradiating red beard, was pushing before him a barrow, which was ablaze with incomparable flowers. There were splendid specimens of almost every order, but the Major's own favourite pansies predominated. The Major stopped and fell into conversation, and then into bargaining. He treated the man after the manner of collectors and other mad men, that is to say, he carefully and with a sort of anguish selected the best roots from the less excellent, praised some, disparaged others, made a subtle scale ranging from a thrilling worth and rarity to a degraded insignificance, and then bought them all. The man was just pushing off his barrow when he stopped and came close to the Major.

'I'll tell you what, sir,' he said. 'If you're interested in them things, you just get on to that wall.'

'On the wall!' cried the scandalised Major, whose conventional soul quailed within him at the thought of such fantastic trespass.

'Finest show of yellow pansies in England in that there garden, sir,' hissed the tempter. 'I'll help you up, sir.'

How it happened no one will ever know but that positive enthusiasm of the Major's life triumphed over all its negative traditions, and with an easy leap and swing that showed that he was in no need of physical assistance, he stood on the wall at the end of the strange garden. The second after, the flapping of the frock-coat at his knees made him feel inexpressibly a fool. But the next instant all such trifling sentiments were swallowed up by the most appalling shock of surprise the old soldier had ever felt in all his bold and wandering existence. His eyes fell upon the garden, and there across a large bed in the centre of the lawn was a vast pattern of pansies; they were splendid flowers, but for once it was not their horticultural aspects that Major Brown beheld, for the pansies were arranged in gigantic capital letters so as to form the sentence: DEATH TO MAJOR BROWN.

A kindly looking old man, with white whiskers, was watering them. Brown looked sharply back at the road behind him; the man with the barrow had suddenly vanished. Then he looked again at the lawn with its incredible inscription. Another man might have thought he had gone mad, but Brown did not. When romantic ladies gushed over his VC and his military exploits, he sometimes felt himself to be a painfully prosaic person, but by the same token he knew he was incurably sane. Another man, again, might have thought himself a victim of a passing practical joke, but Brown could not easily believe this. He knew from his own quaint learning that the garden arrangement was an elaborate and expensive one; he thought it extravagantly improbable that anyone would pour out money like water for a joke against him. Having no explanation whatever to offer, he admitted the fact to himself, like a clear-headed man, and waited as he would have done in the presence of a man with six legs.

At this moment the stout old man with white whiskers looked up, and the watering can fell from his hand, shooting a swirl of water down the gravel path.

'Who on earth are you?' he gasped, trembling violently.

'I am Major Brown,' said that individual, who was always cool in the hour of action.

The old man gaped helplessly like some monstrous fish. At last he stammered wildly, 'Come down – come down here!'

'At your service,' said the Major, and alighted at a bound on the grass beside him, without disarranging his silk hat.

The old man turned his broad back and set off at a sort of waddling run towards the house, followed with swift steps by the Major. His guide led him through the back passages of a gloomy, but gorgeously appointed house, until they reached the door of the front room. Then the old man turned with a face of apoplectic terror dimly showing in the twilight.

'For heaven's sake,' he said, 'don't mention jackals.'

Then he threw open the door, releasing a burst of red lamp-light, and ran downstairs with a clatter.

The Major stepped into a rich, glowing room, full of red copper, and peacock and purple hangings, hat in hand. He had the finest manners in the world, and, though mystified, was not in the least embarrassed to see that the only occupant was a lady, sitting by the window, looking out.

'Madam,' he said, bowing simply, 'I am Major Brown.'

'Sit down,' said the lady; but she did not turn her head.

She was a graceful, green-clad figure, with fiery red hair and a flavour of Bedford Park.[6] 'You have come, I suppose,' she said mournfully, 'to tax me about the hateful title deeds.'

'I have come, madam,' he said, 'to know what is the matter. To know why my name is written across your garden. Not amicably either.'

He spoke grimly, for the thing had hit him. It is impossible to describe the effect produced on the mind by that quiet and sunny garden scene, the frame for a stunning and brutal person-ality. The evening air was still, and the grass was golden in the place where the little flowers he studied cried to heaven for his blood.

'You know I must not turn round,' said the lady; 'every after-noon till the stroke of six I must keep my face turned to the street.'

Some queer and unusual inspiration made the prosaic soldier resolute to accept these outrageous riddles without surprise.

'It is almost six,' he said; and even as he spoke the barbaric copper clock upon the wall clanged the first stroke of the hour.

At the sixth the lady sprang up and turned on the Major one of the queerest and yet most attractive faces he had ever seen in his life; open, and yet tantalising, the face of an elf.

'That makes the third year I have waited,' she cried. 'This is an anniversary. The waiting almost makes one wish the frightful thing would happen once and for all.'

And even as she spoke, a sudden rending cry broke the stillness. From low down on the pavement of the dim street (it was already twilight) a voice cried out with a raucous and merciless distinctness:

'Major Brown, Major Brown, where does the jackal dwell?'

Brown was decisive and silent in action. He strode to the front door and looked out. There was no sign of life in the blue gloaming of the street, where one or two lamps were beginning to light their lemon sparks. On returning, he found the lady in green trembling.

'It is the end,' she cried, with shaking lips; 'it may be death for both of us. Whenever – '

But even as she spoke her speech was cloven by another hoarse proclamation from the dark street, again horribly articulate.

'Major Brown, Major Brown, how did the jackal die?'

Brown dashed out of the door and down the steps, but again he was frustrated; there was no figure in sight, and the street was far too long and empty for the shouter to have run away. Even the rational Major was a little shaken as he returned in a certain time to the drawing room. Scarcely had he done so than the terrific voice came:

'Major Brown, Major Brown, where did – '

Brown was in the street almost at a bound, and he was in time – in time to see something which at first glance froze the blood. The cries appeared to come from a decapitated head resting on the pavement.

The next moment the pale Major understood. It was the head of a man thrust through the coal-hole in the street. The next moment, again, it had vanished, and Major Brown turned to thelady. 'Where's your coal-cellar?' he said, and stepped out into the passage.

She looked at him with wild grey eyes. 'You will not go down,' she cried, 'alone, into the dark hole, with that beast?'

'Is this the way?' replied Brown, and descended the kitchen stairs three at a time. He flung open the door of a black cavity and stepped in, feeling in his pocket for matches. As his right hand was thus occupied, a pair of great slimy hands came out of the darkness, hands clearly belonging to a man of gigantic stature, and seized him by the back of the head. They forced him down, down in the suffocating darkness, a brutal image of destiny. But the Major's head, though upside down, was perfectly clear and intellectual. He gave quietly under the pressure until he had slid down almost to his hands and knees. Then finding the knees of the invisible monster within a foot of him, he simply put out one of his long, bony, and skilful hands, and gripping the leg by a muscle pulled it off the ground and laid the huge living man, with a crash, along the floor. He strove to rise, but Brown was on top like a cat. They rolled over and over. Big as the man was, he had evidently now no desire but to escape; he made sprawls hither and thither to get past the Major to the door, but that tenacious person had him hard by the coat collar and hung with the other hand to a beam. At length there came a strain in holding back this human bull, a strain under which Brown expected his hand to rend and part from the arm. But something else rent and parted; and the dim fat figure of the giant vanished out of the cellar, leaving the torn coat in the Major's hand; the only fruit of his adventure and the only clue to the mystery. For when he went up and out at the front door, the lady, the rich hangings, and the whole equipment of the house had disappeared. It had only bare boards and whitewashed walls.

'The lady was in the conspiracy, of course,' said Rupert, nodding. Major Brown turned brick red. 'I beg your pardon,' he said, 'I think not.'

Rupert raised his eyebrows and looked at him for a moment, but said nothing. When next he spoke he asked:

'Was there anything in the pockets of the coat?'

'There was sevenpence halfpenny in coppers and a three-penny bit,' said the Major carefully; 'there was a cigarette-holder, a piece of string, and this letter,' and he laid it on the table. It ran as follows:

Dear Mr Plover,

I am annoyed to hear that some delay has occurred in the arrangements re Major Brown. Please see that he is attacked as per arrangement tomorrow. The coal-cellar, of course.

Yours faithfully, P.G. Northover.

Rupert Grant was leaning forward listening with hawklike eyes. He cut in:

'Is it dated from anywhere?'

'No – oh, yes!' replied Brown, glancing upon the paper; '14 Tanner's Court, North – '

Rupert sprang up and struck his hands together.

'Then why are we hanging here? Let's get along. Basil, lend me your revolver.'

Basil was staring into the embers like a man in a trance; and it was some time before he answered:

'I don't think you'll need it.'

'Perhaps not,' said Rupert, getting into his fur coat. 'One never knows. But going down a dark court to see criminals – '

'Do you think they are criminals?' asked his brother.

Rupert laughed stoutly. 'Giving orders to a subordinate to strangle a harmless stranger in a coal-cellar may strike you as a very blameless experiment, but – '

'Do you think they wanted to strangle the Major?' asked Basil, in the same distant and monotonous voice.

'My dear fellow, you've been asleep. Look at the letter.'

'I am looking at the letter,' said the mad judge calmly; though, as a matter of fact, he was looking at the fire. 'I don't think it's the sort of letter one criminal would write to another.'

'My dear boy, you are glorious,' cried Rupert, turning round, with laughter in his blue bright eyes. 'Your methods amaze me. Why, there is the letter. It is written, and it does give orders for a crime. You might as well say that the Nelson Column was not at all the sort of thing that was likely to be set up in Trafalgar Square.'

Basil Grant shook all over with a sort of silent laughter, but did not otherwise move.

'That's rather good,' he said; 'but, of course, logic like that's not what is really wanted. It's a question of spiritual atmosphere. It's not a criminal letter.'

'It is. It's a matter of fact,' cried the other in an agony of reasonableness.

'Facts,' murmured Basil, like one mentioning some strange, far-off animals, 'how facts obscure the truth. I may be silly – in fact, I'm off my head – but I never could believe in that man – what's his name, in those capital stories? – Sherlock Holmes. Every detail points to something, certainly; but generally to the wrong thing. Facts point in all directions, it seems to me, like the thousands of twigs on a tree. It's only the life of the tree that has unity and goes up – only the green blood that springs, like a fountain, at the stars.'

'But what the deuce else can the letter be but criminal?'

'We have eternity to stretch our legs in,' replied the mystic. 'It can be an infinity of things. I haven't seen any of them – I've only seen the letter. I look at that, and say it's not criminal.'

'Then what's the origin of it?'

'I haven't the vaguest idea.'

'Then why don't you accept the ordinary explanation?'

Basil continued for a little to glare at the coals, and seemed collecting his thoughts in a humble and even painful way. Then he said:

'Suppose you went out into the moonlight. Suppose you passed through silent, silvery streets and squares until you came into an open and deserted space, set with a few monuments, and you beheld one dressed as a ballet girl dancing in the argent glimmer. And suppose you looked, and saw it was a man disguised. And suppose you looked again, and saw it was Lord Kitchener.[7] What would you think?'

He paused a moment, and went on:

'You could not adopt the ordinary explanation. The ordinary explanation of putting on singular clothes is that you look nice in them; you would not think that Lord Kitchener dressed up like a ballet girl out of ordinary personal vanity. You would think it much more likely that he inherited a dancing madness from a great grandmother; or had been hypnotised at a seance; or threatened by a secret society with death if he refused the ordeal. With Baden-Powell,[8] say, it might be a bet – but not with Kitchener. I should know all that, because in my public days I knew him quite well. So I know that letter quite well, and criminals quite well. It's not a criminal's letter. It's all atmospheres.' And he closed his eyes and passed his hand over his forehead.

Rupert and the Major were regarding him with a mixture of respect and pity. The former said:

'Well, I'm going, anyhow, and shall continue to think – until your spiritual mystery turns up – that a man who sends a note recommending a crime, that is, actually a crime that is actually carried out, at least tentatively, is, in all probability, a little casual in his moral tastes. Can I have that revolver?'

'Certainly,' said Basil, getting up. 'But I am coming with you.' And he flung an old cape or cloak round him, and took a swordstick from the corner.

'You!' said Rupert, with some surprise, 'you scarcely ever leave your hole to look at anything on the face of the earth.'

Basil fitted on a formidable old white hat.

'I scarcely ever,' he said, with an unconscious and colossal arrogance, 'hear of anything on the face of the earth that I do not understand at once, without going to see it.'

And he led the way out into the purple night.

We four swung along the flaring Lambeth streets, across Westminster Bridge, and along the Embankment in the direction of that part of Fleet Street which contained Tanner's Court. The erect, black figure of Major Brown, seen from behind, was a quaint contrast to the houndlike stoop and flapping mantle of young Rupert Grant, who adopted, with childlike delight, all the dramatic poses of the detective of fiction. The finest among his many fine qualities was his boyish appetite for the colour and poetry of London. Basil, who walked behind, with his face turned blindly to the stars, had the look of a somnambulist.

Rupert paused at the corner of Tanner's Court, with a quiver of delight at danger, and gripped Basil's revolver in his great-coat pocket.

'Shall we go in now?' he asked.

'Not get police?' asked Major Brown, glancing sharply up and down the street.

'I am not sure,' answered Rupert, knitting his brows. 'Of course, it's quite clear, the thing's all crooked. But there are three of us, and – '

'I shouldn't get the police,' said Basil in a queer voice. Rupert glanced at him and stared hard.

'Basil,' he cried, 'you're trembling. What's the matter – are you afraid?'

'Cold, perhaps,' said the Major, eyeing him. There was no doubt that he was shaking.

At last, after a few moments' scrutiny, Rupert broke into a curse.

'You're laughing,' he cried. 'I know that confounded, silent, shaky laugh of yours. What the deuce is the amusement, Basil? Here we are, all three of us, within a yard of a den of ruffians – '

'But I shouldn't call the police,' said Basil. 'We four heroes are quite equal to a host,' and he continued to quake with his mysterious mirth.

Rupert turned with impatience and strode swiftly down the court, the rest of us following. When he reached the door of No. 14 he turned abruptly, the revolver glittering in his hand.

'Stand close,' he said in the voice of a commander. 'The scoundrel may be attempting an escape at this moment. We must fling open the door and rush in.'

The four of us cowered instantly under the archway, rigid, except for the old judge and his convulsion of merriment.

'Now,' hissed Rupert Grant, turning his pale face and burning eyes suddenly over his shoulder, 'when I say "Four", follow me with a rush. If I say "Hold him", pin the fellows down, whoever they are. If I say "Stop", stop. I shall say that if there are more than three. If they attack us I shall empty my revolver on them. Basil, have your swordstick ready. Now – one, two, three, four!'

With the sound of the word the door burst open, and we fell into the room like an invasion, only to stop dead.

The room, which was an ordinary and neatly appointed office, appeared, at the first glance, to be empty. But on a second and more careful glance, we saw seated behind a very large desk with pigeonholes and drawers of bewildering multiplicity, a small man with a black waxed moustache, and the air of a very average clerk, writing hard. He looked up as we came to a standstill.

'Did you knock?' he asked pleasantly. 'I am sorry if I did not hear. What can I do for you?'

There was a doubtful pause, and then, by general consent, the Major himself, the victim of the outrage, stepped forward.

The letter was in his hand, and he looked unusually grim.

'Is your name P.G. Northover?' he asked.

'That is my name,' replied the other, smiling.

'I think,' said Major Brown, with an increase in the dark glow of his face, 'that this letter was written by you.' And with a loud clap he struck open the letter on the desk with his clenched fist. The man called Northover looked at it with unaffected interest and merely nodded.

'Well, sir,' said the Major, breathing hard, 'what about that?'

'What about it, precisely,' said the man with the moustache.

'I am Major Brown,' said that gentleman sternly.

Northover bowed. 'Pleased to meet you, sir. What have you to say to me?'

'Say!' cried the Major, loosing a sudden tempest; 'why, I want this confounded thing settled. I want – '

'Certainly, sir,' said Northover, jumping up with a slight elevation of the eyebrows. 'Will you take a chair for a moment.' And he pressed an electric bell just above him, which thrilled and tinkled in a room beyond. The Major put his hand on the back of the chair offered him, but stood chafing and beating the floor with his polished boot.

The next moment an inner glass door was opened, and a fair, weedy, young man, in a frock-coat, entered from within.

'Mr Hopson,' said Northover, 'this is Major Brown. Will you please finish that thing for him I gave you this morning and bring it in?'

'Yes, sir,' said Mr Hopson, and vanished like lightning.

'You will excuse me, gentlemen,' said the egregious Northover, with his radiant smile, 'if I continue to work until Mr Hopson is ready. I have some books that must be cleared up before I get away on my holiday tomorrow. And we all like a whiff of the country, don't we? Ha! ha!'

The criminal took up his pen with a childlike laugh, and a silence ensued; a placid and busy silence on the part of Mr P.G. Northover; a raging silence on the part of everybody else.

At length the scratching of Northover's pen in the stillness was mingled with a knock at the door, almost simultaneous with the turning of the handle, and Mr Hopson came in again with the same silent rapidity, placed a paper before his principal, and disappeared again.

The man at the desk pulled and twisted his spiky moustache for a few moments as he ran his eye up and down the paper presented to him. He took up his pen, with a slight, instantaneous frown, and altered something, muttering – 'Careless.' Then he read it again with the same impenetrable reflectiveness, and finally handed it to the frantic Brown, whose hand was beating the devil's tattoo on the back of the chair.

'I think you will find that all right, Major,' he said briefly.

The Major looked at it; whether he found it all right or not will appear later, but he found it like this:

Major Brown to P.G. Northover.	£.s.d.
January 1, to account rendered	560.00
May 9, to potting and embedding of 200 pansies	200.00

To cost of trolley with flowers	*150.00*
To hiring of man with trolley	*050.00*
To hire of house and garden for one day	*100.00*
To furnishing of room in peacock curtains, copper ornaments, etc.	*300.00*
To salary of Miss Jameson	*100.00*
To salary of Mr Plover	*100.00*
Total	£*1,460.00*

A remittance will oblige.

'What,' said Brown, after a dead pause, and with eyes that seemed slowly rising out of his head. 'What in heaven's name is this?'

'What is it?' repeated Northover, cocking his eyebrow with amusement. 'It's your account, of course.'

'My account!' The Major's ideas appeared to be in a vague stampede. 'My account! And what have I got to do with it?'

'Well,' said Northover, laughing outright, 'naturally I prefer you to pay it.'

The Major's hand was still resting on the back of the chair as the words came. He scarcely stirred otherwise, but he lifted the chair bodily into the air with one hand and hurled it at Northover's head.

The legs crashed against the desk, so that Northover only got a blow on the elbow as he sprang up with clenched fists, only to be seized by the united rush of the rest of us. The chair had fallen clattering on the empty floor.

'Let me go, you scamps,' he shouted. 'Let me – '

'Stand still,' cried Rupert authoritatively. 'Major Brown's action is excusable. The abominable crime you have attempted – '

'A customer has a perfect right,' said Northover hotly, 'to question an alleged overcharge, but, confound it all, not to throw furniture.'

'What, in God's name, do you mean by your customers and overcharges?' shrieked Major Brown, whose keen feminine nature, steady in pain or danger, became almost hysterical in the presence of a long and exasperating mystery. 'Who are you? I've never seen you or your insolent tomfool bills. I know one of your cursed brutes tried to choke me – '

'Mad,' said Northover, gazing blankly round; 'all of them mad. I didn't know they travelled in quartets.'

'Enough of this prevarication,' said Rupert; 'your crimes are discovered. A policeman is stationed at the corner of the court. Though only a private detective myself, I will take the responsibility of telling you that anything you say – '

'Mad,' repeated Northover, with a weary air.

And at this moment, for the first time, there struck in among them the strange, sleepy voice of Basil Grant.

'Major Brown,' he said, 'may I ask you a question?'

The Major turned his head with an increased bewilderment.

'You?' he cried; 'certainly, Mr Grant.'

'Can you tell me,' said the mystic, with sunken head and lowering brow, as he traced a pattern in the dust with his swordstick, 'can you tell me what was the name of the man who lived in your house before you?'

The unhappy Major was only faintly more disturbed by this last and futile irrelevancy, and he answered vaguely:

'Yes, I think so; a man named Gurney something – a name with a hyphen – Gurney-Brown; that was it.'

'And when did the house change hands?' said Basil, looking up sharply. His strange eyes were burning brilliantly.

'I came in last month,' said the Major.

And at the mere word the criminal Northover suddenly fell into his great office chair and shouted with a volleying laughter.

'Oh! it's too perfect – it's too exquisite,' he gasped, beating the arms with his fists. He was laughing deafeningly; Basil Grant was laughing voicelessly; and the rest of us only felt that our heads were like weathercocks in a whirlwind.

'Confound it, Basil,' said Rupert, stamping. 'If you don't want me to go mad and blow your metaphysical brains out, tell me what all this means.'

Northover rose.

'Permit me, sir, to explain,' he said. 'And, first of all, permit me to apologise to you, Major Brown, for a most abominable and unpardonable blunder, which has caused you menace and inconvenience, in which, if you will allow me to say so, you have behaved with astonishing courage and dignity. Of course you need not trouble about the bill. We will stand the loss.' And, tearing the paper across, he flung the halves into the waste-paper basket and bowed.

Poor Brown's face was still a picture of distraction. 'But I don't even begin to understand,' he cried. 'What bill? what blunder? what loss?'

Mr P.G. Northover advanced in the centre of the room, thoughtfully, and with a great deal of unconscious dignity. On closer consideration, there were apparent about him other things beside a screwed moustache, especially a lean, sallow face, hawklike, and not without a careworn intelligence. Then he looked up abruptly.

'Do you know where you are, Major?' he said.

'God knows I don't,' said the warrior, with fervour.

'You are standing,' replied Northover, 'in the office of the Adventure and Romance Agency, Limited.'

'And what's that?' blankly enquired Brown.

The man of business leaned over the back of the chair, and fixed his dark eyes on the other's face.

'Major,' said he, 'did you ever, as you walked along the empty street upon some idle afternoon, feel the utter hunger for something to happen – something, in the splendid words of Walt Whitman: "Something pernicious and dread; something far removed from a puny and pious life; something unproved; something in a trance; something loosed from its anchorage, and driving free." Did you ever feel that?'

'Certainly not,' said the Major shortly.

'Then I must explain with more elaboration,' said Mr Northover, with a sigh. 'The Adventure and Romance Agency has been started to meet a great modern desire. On every side, in conversation and in literature, we hear of the desire for a larger theatre of events, for something to waylay us and lead us splendidly astray. Now the man who feels this desire for a varied life pays a yearly or a quarterly sum to the Adventure and Romance Agency; in return, the Adventure and Romance Agency undertakes to surround him with startling and weird events. As a man is leaving his front door, an excited sweep approaches him and assures him of a plot against his life; he gets into a cab, and is driven to an opium den; he receives a mysterious telegram or a dramatic visit, and is immediately in a vortex of incidents. A very picturesque and moving story is first written by one of the staff of distinguished novelists who are at present hard at work in the adjoining room. Yours, Major Brown (designed by our Mr Grigsby), I consider peculiarly forcible and pointed; it is almost a pity you did not see the end of it. I need scarcely explain further the monstrous mistake. Your predecessor in your present house, Mr Gurney-Brown, was a subscriber to our agency, and our foolish clerks, ignoring alike the dignity of the hyphen and the glory of military rank, positively imagined that Major Brown and Mr Gurney-Brown were the same person. Thus you were suddenly hurled into the middle of another man's story.'

'How on earth does the thing work?' asked Rupert Grant, with bright and fascinated eyes.

'We believe that we are doing a noble work,' said Northover warmly. 'It has continually struck us that there is no element in modern life that is more lamentable than the fact that the modern man has to seek all artistic existence in a sedentary state. If he wishes to float into fairyland, he reads a book; if he wishes to dash into the thick of battle, he reads a book; if he wishes to soar into heaven, he reads a book; if he wishes to slide down the banisters, he reads a book. We give him these visions, but we give him exercise at the same time, the necessity of leaping from wall to wall, of fighting strange gentlemen, of running down long streets from pursuers – all healthy and pleasant exercises. We give him a glimpse of that great morning world of Robin Hood or the knights errant, when one great game was played under the splendid sky. We give him back his childhood, that godlike time when we can act stories, be our own heroes, and at the same instant dance and dream.'

Basil gazed at him curiously. The most singular psychological discovery had been reserved to the end, for as the little businessman ceased speaking he had the blazing eyes of a fanatic.

Major Brown received the explanation with complete simplicity and good humour.

'Of course; awfully dense, sir,' he said. 'No doubt at all, the scheme excellent. But I don't think – ' He paused a moment, and looked dreamily out of the window. 'I don't think you will find me in it. Somehow, when one's seen – seen the thing itself, you know – blood and men screaming, one feels about having a little house and a little hobby; in the Bible, you know, "There remaineth a rest".'

Northover bowed. Then after a pause he said:

'Gentlemen, may I offer you my card. If any of the rest of you desire, at any time, to communicate with me, despite Major Brown's view of the matter – '

'I should be obliged for your card, sir,' said the Major, in his abrupt but courteous voice. 'Pay for chair.'

The agent of Romance and Adventure handed his card, laughing.

It ran, 'P.G. Northover, BA, CQT, Adventure and Romance Agency, 14 Tanner's Court, Fleet Street.'

'What on earth is "CQT"?' asked Rupert Grant, looking over the Major's shoulder.

'Don't you know?' returned Northover. 'Haven't you ever heard of the Club of Queer Trades?'

'There seems to be a confounded lot of funny things we haven't heard of,' said the little Major reflectively. 'What's this one?'

'The Club of Queer Trades is a society consisting exclusively of people who have invented some new and curious way of making money. I was one of the earliest members.'

'You deserve to be,' said Basil, taking up his great white hat, with a smile, and speaking for the last time that evening.

When they had passed out the Adventure and Romance agent wore a queer smile, as he trod down the fire and locked up his desk. 'A fine chap, that Major; when one hasn't a touch of the poet one stands some chance of being a poem. But to think of such a clockwork little creature of all people getting into the nets of one of Grigsby's tales,' and he laughed out aloud in the silence.

Just as the laugh echoed away, there came a sharp knock at the door. An owlish head, with dark moustaches, was thrust in, with deprecating and somewhat absurd enquiry.

'What! back again, Major?' cried Northover in surprise. 'What can I do for you?'

The Major shuffled feverishly into the room.

'It's horribly absurd,' he said. 'Something must have got started in me that I never knew before. But upon my soul I feel the most desperate desire to know the end of it all.'

'The end of it all?'

'Yes,' said the Major. '"Jackals", and the title deeds, and "Death to Major Brown".'

The agent's face grew grave, but his eyes were amused.

'I am terribly sorry, Major,' said he, 'but what you ask is impossible. I don't know anyone I would sooner oblige than you; but the rules of the agency are strict. The Adventures are confidential; you are an outsider; I am not allowed to let you know an inch more than I can help. I do hope you understand – '

'There is no one,' said Brown, 'who understands discipline better than I do. Thank you very much. Goodnight.'

And the little man withdrew for the last time.

He married Miss Jameson, the lady with the red hair and the green garments. She was an actress, employed (with many others) by the Romance Agency; and her marriage with the prim old veteran caused some stir in her languid and intellectu-alised set. She always replied very quietly that she had met scores of men who acted splendidly in the charades provided for them by Northover, but that she had only met one man who went down into a coal-cellar when he really thought it contained a murderer.

The Major and she are living as happily as birds, in an absurd villa, and the former has taken to smoking. Otherwise he is unchanged – except, perhaps, there are moments when, alert and full of feminine unselfishness as the Major is by nature, he falls into a trance of abstraction. Then his wife recognises with a concealed smile, by the blind look in his blue eyes, that he is wondering what were the title deeds, and why he was not allowed to mention jackals. But, like so many old soldiers, Brown is religious, and believes that he will realise the rest of those purple adventures in a better world.

2

The Painful Fall of a Great Reputation

Basil Grant and I were talking one day in what is perhaps the most perfect place for talking on earth – the top of a tolerably deserted tramcar. To talk on the top of a hill is superb, but to talk on the top of a flying hill is a fairy tale.

The vast blank space of North London was flying by; the very pace gave us a sense of its immensity and its meanness. It was, as it were, a base infinitude, a squalid eternity, and we felt the real horror of the poor parts of London, the horror that is so totally missed and misrepresented by the sensational novelists who depict it as being a matter of narrow streets, filthy houses, criminals and maniacs, and dens of vice. In a narrow street, in a den of vice, you do not expect civilisation, you do not expect order. But the horror of this was the fact that there was civilisation, that there was order, but that civilisation only showed its morbidity, and order only its monotony. No one would say, in going through a criminal slum, 'I see no statues. I notice no cathedrals.' But here there were public buildings; only they were mostly lunatic asylums. Here there were statues; only they were mostly statues of railway engineers and philanthropists – two dingy classes of men united by their common contempt for the people. Here there were churches; only they were the churches of dim and erratic sects, Agapemonites[9] or Irvingites.[10] Here, above all, there were broad roads and vast crossings and tramway lines and hospitals and all the real marks of civilisation. But though one never knew, in one sense, what one would see next, there was one thing we knew we should not see – anything really great, central, of the first class, anything that humanity had adored. And with revulsion indescribable our emotions returned, I think, to those really close and crooked entries, to those really mean streets, to those genuine slums which lie round the Thames and the City, in which nevertheless a real possibility remains that at any chance corner the great cross of the great cathedral of Wren[11] may strike down the street like a thunderbolt.

'But you must always remember also,' said Grant to me, in his heavy abstracted way, when I had urged this view, 'that the very vileness of the life of these ordered plebeian places bears witness to the victory of the human soul. I agree with you. I agree that they have to live in something worse than barbarism. They have to live in a fourth-rate civilisation. But yet I am practically certain that the majority of people here are good people. And being good is an adventure far more violent and daring than sailing round the world. Besides – '

'Go on,' I said.

No answer came.

'Go on,' I said, looking up.

The big blue eyes of Basil Grant were standing out of his head and he was paying no attention to me. He was staring over the side of the tram.

'What is the matter?' I asked, peering over also.

'It is very odd,' said Grant at last, grimly, 'that I should have been caught out like this at the very moment of my optimism. I said all these people were good, and there is the wickedest man in England.'

'Where?' I asked, leaning over further, 'where?'

'Oh, I was right enough,' he went on, in that strange continuous and sleepy tone which always angered his hearers at acute moments, 'I was right enough when I said all these people were good. They are heroes; they are saints. Now and then they may perhaps steal a spoon or two; they may beat a wife or two with the poker. But they are saints all the same; they are angels; they are robed in white; they are clad with wings and haloes – at any rate compared to that man.'

'Which man?' I cried again, and then my eye caught the figure at which Basil's bull's eyes were glaring.

He was a slim, smooth person, passing very quickly among the quickly passing crowd, but though there was nothing about him sufficient to attract a startled notice, there was quite enough to demand a curious consideration when once that notice was attracted. He wore a black top-hat, but there was enough in it of those strange curves whereby the decadent artist of the eighties tried to turn the top-hat into something as rhythmic as an Etruscan vase. His hair, which was largely grey, was curled with the instinct of one who appreciated the gradual beauty of grey and silver. The rest of his face was oval and, I thought, rather oriental; he had two black tufts of moustache.

'What has he done?' I asked.

'I am not sure of the details,' said Grant, 'but his besetting sin is a desire to intrigue to the disadvantage of others. Probably he has adopted some imposture or other to effect his plan.'

'What plan?' I asked. 'If you know all about him, why don't you tell me why he is the wickedest man in England? What is his name?'

Basil Grant stared at me for some moments.

'I think you've made a mistake in my meaning,' he said. 'I don't know his name. I never saw him before in my life.'

'Never saw him before!' I cried, with a kind of anger; 'then what in heaven's name do you mean by saying that he is the wickedest man in England?'

'I meant what I said,' said Basil Grant calmly. 'The moment I saw that man, I saw all these people stricken with a sudden and splendid innocence. I saw that while all ordinary poor men in the streets were being themselves, he was not being himself. I saw that all the men in these slums, cadgers, pickpockets, hooligans, are all, in the deepest sense, trying to be good. And I saw that that man was trying to be evil.'

'But if you never saw him before – ' I began.

'In God's name, look at his face,' cried out Basil in a voice that startled the driver. 'Look at the eyebrows. They mean that infernal pride which made Satan so proud that he sneered even at heaven when he was one of the first angels in it. Look at his moustaches, they are so grown as to insult humanity. In the name of the sacred heavens, look at his hair. In the name of God and the stars, look at his hat.'

I stirred uncomfortably.

'But, after all,' I said, 'this is very fanciful – perfectly absurd. Look at the mere facts. You have never seen the man before, you – '

'Oh, the mere facts,' he cried out in a kind of despair. 'The mere facts! Do you really admit – are you still so sunk in superstitions, so clinging to dim and prehistoric altars, that you believe in facts? Do you not trust an immediate impression?'

'Well, an immediate impression may be,' I said, 'a little less practical than facts.'

'Bosh,' he said. 'On what else is the whole world run but immediate impressions? What is more practical? My friend, the philosophy of this world may be founded on facts, its business is run on spiritual impressions and atmospheres. Why do you refuse or accept a clerk? Do you measure his skull? Do you read up his physiological state in a handbook? Do you go upon facts at all? Not a scrap. You accept a clerk who may save your business – you refuse a clerk that may rob your till, entirely upon those immediate mystical impressions under the pressure of which I pronounce, with a perfect sense of certainty and sincerity, that that man walking in that street beside us is a humbug and a villain of some kind.'

'You always put things well,' I said, 'but, of course, such things cannot immediately be put to the test.'

Basil sprang up straight and swayed with the swaying car.

'Let us get off and follow him,' he said. 'I bet you five pounds it will turn out as I say.'

And with a scuttle, a jump and a run, we were off the car.

The man with the curved silver hair and the curved Eastern face walked along for some time, his long splendid frock-coat flying behind him. Then he swung sharply out of the great glaring road and disappeared down an ill-lit alley. We swung silently after him.

'This is an odd turning for a man of that kind to take,' I said.

'A man of what kind?' asked my friend.

'Well,' I said, 'a man with that kind of expression and those boots. I thought it rather odd, to tell the truth, that he should be in this part of the world at all.'

'Ah, yes,' said Basil, and said no more.

We tramped on, looking steadily in front of us. The elegant figure, like the figure of a black swan, was silhouetted suddenly against the glare of intermittent gaslight and then swallowed again in night. The intervals between the lights were long, and a fog was thickening the whole city. Our pace, therefore, had become swift and mechanical between the lampposts; but Basil came to a standstill suddenly like a reined horse; I stopped also. We had almost run into the man. A great part of the solid darkness in front of us was the darkness of his body.

At first I thought he had turned to face us. But though we were hardly a yard off he did not realise that we were there. He tapped four times on a very low and dirty door in the dark, crabbed street. A gleam of gas cut the darkness as it opened slowly. We listened intently, but the interview was short and simple and inexplicable as an interview could be. Our exquisite friend handed in what looked like a paper or a card and said:

'At once. Take a cab.'

A heavy, deep voice from inside said:

'Right you are.'

And with a click we were in the blackness again, and striding after the striding stranger through a labyrinth of London lanes, the lights just helping us. It was only five o'clock, but winter and the fog had made it like midnight.

'This is really an extraordinary walk for the patent-leather boots,' I repeated.

'I don't know,' said Basil humbly. 'It leads to Berkeley Square.'

As I tramped on I strained my eyes through the dusky atmosphere and tried to make out the direction described. For some ten minutes I wondered and doubted; at the end of that I saw that my friend was right. We were coming to the great dreary spaces of fashionable London – more dreary, one must admit, even than the dreary plebeian spaces.

'This is very extraordinary!' said Basil Grant, as we turned into Berkeley Square.

'What is extraordinary?' I asked. 'I thought you said it was quite natural.'

'I do not wonder,' answered Basil, 'at his walking through nasty streets; I do not wonder at his going to Berkeley Square. But I do wonder at his going to the house of a very good man.'

'What very good man?' I asked with exasperation.

'The operation of time is a singular one,' he said with his imperturbable irrelevancy. 'It is not a true statement of the case to say that I have forgotten my career when I was a judge and a public man. I remember it all vividly, but it is like remembering some novel. But fifteen years ago I knew this square as well as Lord Rosebery[12] does, and a confounded long sight better than that man who is going up the steps of old Beaumont's house.'

'Who is old Beaumont?' I asked irritably.

'A perfectly good fellow. Lord Beaumont of Foxwood – don't you know his name? He is a man of transparent sincerity, a nobleman who does more work than a navvy, a socialist, an anarchist, I don't know what; anyhow, he's a philosopher and philanthropist.

I admit he has the slight disadvantage of being, beyond all question, off his head. He has that real disadvantage which has arisen out of the modern worship of progress and novelty; and he thinks anything odd and new must be an advance. If you went to him and proposed to eat your grandmother, he would agree with you, so long as you put it on hygienic and public grounds, as a cheap alternative to cremation. So long as you progress fast enough it seems a matter of indifference to him whether you are progressing to the stars or the devil. So his house is filled with an endless succession of literary and political fashions; men who wear long hair because it is romantic; men who wear short hair because it is medical; men who walk on their feet only to exercise their hands; and men who walk on their hands for fear of tiring their feet. But though the inhabitants of his salons are generally fools, like himself, they are almost always, like himself, good men. I am really surprised to see a criminal enter there.'

'My good fellow,' I said firmly, striking my foot on the pavement, 'the truth of this affair is very simple. To use your own eloquent language, you have the "slight disadvantage" of being off your head. You see a total stranger in a public street; you choose to start certain theories about his eyebrows. You then treat him as a burglar because he enters an honest man's door. The thing is too monstrous. Admit that it is, Basil, and come home with me. Though these people are still having tea, yet with the distance we have to go, we shall be late for dinner.'

Basil's eyes were shining in the twilightlike lamps.

'I thought,' he said, 'that I had outlived vanity.'

'What do you want now?' I cried.

'I want,' he cried out, 'what a girl wants when she wears her new frock; I want what a boy wants when he goes in for a clanging match with a monitor – I want to show somebody what a fine fellow I am. I am as right about that man as I am about your having a hat on your head. You say it cannot be tested.

36

I say it can. I will take you to see my old friend Beaumont. He is a delightful man to know.'

'Do you really mean – ?' I began.

'I will apologise,' he said calmly, 'for our not being dressed for a call,' and walking across the vast misty square, he walked up the dark stone steps and rang at the bell.

A severe servant in black and white opened the door to us: on receiving my friend's name his manner passed in a flash from astonishment to respect. We were ushered into the house very quickly, but not so quickly but that our host, a white-haired man with a fiery face, came out quickly to meet us.

'My dear fellow,' he cried, shaking Basil's hand again and again, 'I have not seen you for years. Have you been – er – ' he said, rather wildly, 'have you been in the country?'

'Not for all that time,' answered Basil, smiling. 'I have long given up my official position, my dear Philip, and have been living in a deliberate retirement. I hope I do not come at an inopportune moment.'

'An inopportune moment,' cried the ardent gentleman. 'You come at the most opportune moment I could imagine. Do you know who is here?'

'I do not,' answered Grant, with gravity. Even as he spoke a roar of laughter came from the inner room.

'Basil,' said Lord Beaumont solemnly, 'I have Wimpole here.'

'And who is Wimpole?'

'Basil,' cried the other, 'you must have been in the country. You must have been in the antipodes. You must have been in the moon. Who is Wimpole? Who was Shakespeare?'

'As to who Shakespeare was,' answered my friend placidly, 'my views go no further than thinking that he was not Bacon. More probably he was Mary Queen of Scots. But as to who Wimpole is – ' and his speech also was cloven with a roar of laughter from within.

'Wimpole!' cried Lord Beaumont, in a sort of ecstasy. 'Haven't you heard of the great modern wit? My dear fellow, he has turned conversation, I do not say into an art – for that, perhaps, it always was but into a great art, like the statuary of Michael Angelo – an art of masterpieces. His repartees, my good friend, startle one like a man shot dead. They are final; they are – '

Again there came the hilarious roar from the room, and almost with the very noise of it, a big, panting apoplectic old gentleman came out of the inner house into the hall where we were standing.

'Now, my dear chap,' began Lord Beaumont hastily.

'I tell you, Beaumont, I won't stand it,' exploded the large old gentleman. 'I won't be made game of by a twopenny literary adventurer like that. I won't be made a guy. I won't – '

'Come, come,' said Beaumont feverishly. 'Let me introduce you. This is Mr Justice Grant – that is, Mr Grant. Basil, I am sure you have heard of Sir Walter Cholmondeliegh.'

'Who has not?' asked Grant, and bowed to the worthy old baronet, eyeing him with some curiosity. He was hot and heavy in his momentary anger, but even that could not conceal the noble though opulent outline of his face and body, the florid white hair, the Roman nose, the body stalwart though corpulent, the chin aristocratic though double. He was a magnificent courtly gentleman; so much of a gentleman that he could show an unquestionable weakness of anger without altogether losing dignity; so much of a gentleman that even his faux pas were well-bred.

'I am distressed beyond expression, Beaumont,' he said gruffly, 'to fail in respect to these gentlemen, and even more especially to fail in it in your house. But it is not you or they that are in any way concerned, but that flashy half-caste jackanapes – '

At this moment a young man with a twist of red moustache and a sombre air came out of the inner room. He also did not seem to be greatly enjoying the intellectual banquet within.

'I think you remember my friend and secretary, Mr Drummond,' said Lord Beaumont, turning to Grant, 'even if you only remember him as a schoolboy.'

'Perfectly,' said the other. Mr Drummond shook hands pleasantly and respectfully, but the cloud was still on his brow. Turning to Sir Walter Cholmondeliegh, he said:

'I was sent by Lady Beaumont to express her hope that you were not going yet, Sir Walter. She says she has scarcely seen anything of you.'

The old gentleman, still red in the face, had a temporary internal struggle; then his good manners triumphed, and with a gesture of obeisance and a vague utterance of, 'If Lady Beaumont... a lady, of course,' he followed the young man back into the salon. He had scarcely been deposited there half a minute before another peal of laughter told that he had (in all probability) been scored off again.

'Of course, I can excuse dear old Cholmondeliegh,' said Beaumont, as he helped us off with our coats. 'He has not the modern mind.'

'What is the modern mind?' asked Grant.

'Oh, it's enlightened, you know, and progressive – and faces the facts of life seriously.' At this moment another roar of laughter came from within.

'I only ask,' said Basil, 'because of the last two friends of yours who had the modern mind; one thought it wrong to eat fishes and the other thought it right to eat men. I beg your pardon – this way, if I remember right.'

'Do you know,' said Lord Beaumont, with a sort of feverish entertainment, as he trotted after us towards the interior, 'I can never quite make out which side you are on. Sometimes you seem so liberal and sometimes so reactionary. Are you a modern, Basil?'

'No,' said Basil, loudly and cheerfully, as he entered the crowded drawing room.

This caused a slight diversion, and some eyes were turned away from our slim friend with the oriental face for the first time that afternoon. Two people, however, still looked at him. One was the daughter of the house, Muriel Beaumont, who gazed at him with great violet eyes and with the intense and awful thirst of the female upper class for verbal amusement and stimulus. The other was Sir Walter Cholmondeliegh, who looked at him with a still and sullen but unmistakable desire to throw him out of the window.

He sat there, coiled rather than seated on the easy chair; everything from the curves of his smooth limbs to the coils of his silvered hair suggesting the circles of a serpent more than the straight limbs of a man – the unmistakable, splendid serpentine gentleman we had seen walking in North London, his eyes shining with repeated victory.

'What I can't understand, Mr Wimpole,' said Muriel Beaumont eagerly, 'is how you contrive to treat all this so easily. You say things quite philosophical and yet so wildly funny. If I thought of such things, I'm sure I should laugh outright when the thought first came.'

'I agree with Miss Beaumont,' said Sir Walter, suddenly exploding with indignation. 'If I had thought of anything so futile, I should find it difficult to keep my countenance.'

'Difficult to keep your countenance,' cried Mr Wimpole, with an air of alarm; 'oh, do keep your countenance! Keep it in the British Museum.'

Everyone laughed uproariously, as they always do at an already admitted readiness, and Sir Walter, turning suddenly purple, shouted out:

'Do you know who you are talking to, with your confounded tomfooleries?'

'I never talk tomfooleries,' said the other, 'without first knowing my audience.'

Grant walked across the room and tapped the red-moustached secretary on the shoulder. That gentleman was leaning against the wall regarding the whole scene with a great deal of gloom; but, I fancied, with very particular gloom when his eyes fell on the young lady of the house rapturously listening to Wimpole.

'May I have a word with you outside, Drummond?' asked Grant. 'It is about business. Lady Beaumont will excuse us.'

I followed my friend, at his own request, greatly wondering, to this strange external interview. We passed abruptly into a kind of side room out of the hall.

'Drummond,' said Basil sharply, 'there are a great many good people, and a great many sane people here this afternoon. Unfortunately, by a kind of coincidence, all the good people are mad, and all the sane people are wicked. You are the only person I know of here who is honest and has also some common sense. What do you make of Wimpole?'

Mr Secretary Drummond had a pale face and red hair; but at this his face became suddenly as red as his moustache.

'I am not a fair judge of him,' he said.

'Why not?' asked Grant.

'Because I hate him like hell,' said the other, after a long pause and violently.

Neither Grant nor I needed to ask the reason; his glances towards Miss Beaumont and the stranger were sufficiently illuminating. Grant said quietly:

'But before – before you came to hate him, what did you really think of him?'

'I am in a terrible difficulty,' said the young man, and his voice told us, like a clear bell, that he was an honest man. 'If I spoke about him as I feel about him now, I could not trust myself. And I should like to be able to say that when I first saw him I thought he was charming. But again, the fact is I didn't.

41

I hate him, that is my private affair. But I also disapprove of him – really I do believe I disapprove of him quite apart from my private feelings. When first he came, I admit he was much quieter, but I did not like, so to speak, the moral swell of him. Then that jolly old Sir Walter Cholmondeliegh got introduced to us, and this fellow, with his cheap-jack wit, began to score off the old man in the way he does now. Then I felt that he must be a bad lot; it must be bad to fight the old and the kindly. And he fights the poor old chap savagely, unceasingly, as if he hated old age and kindliness. Take, if you want it, the evidence of a prejudiced witness. I admit that I hate the man because a certain person admires him. But I believe that apart from that I should hate the man because old Sir Walter hates him.'

This speech affected me with a genuine sense of esteem and pity for the young man; that is, of pity for him because of his obviously hopeless worship of Miss Beaumont, and of esteem for him because of the direct realistic account of the history of Wimpole which he had given. Still, I was sorry that he seemed so steadily set against the man, and could not help referring it to an instinct of his personal relations, however nobly disguised from himself.

In the middle of these meditations, Grant whispered in my ear what was perhaps the most startling of all interruptions.

'In the name of God, let's get away.'

I have never known exactly in how odd a way this odd old man affected me. I only know that for some reason or other he so affected me that I was, within a few minutes, in the street outside.

'This,' he said, 'is a beastly but amusing affair.'

'What is?' I asked, baldly enough.

'This affair. Listen to me, my old friend. Lord and Lady Beaumont have just invited you and me to a grand dinner party this very night, at which Mr Wimpole will be in all his glory.

Well, there is nothing very extraordinary about that. The extra-ordinary thing is that we are not going.'

'Well, really,' I said, 'it is already six o'clock and I doubt if we could get home and dress. I see nothing extraordinary in the fact that we are not going.'

'Don't you?' said Grant. 'I'll bet you'll see something extra-ordinary in what we're doing instead.'

I looked at him blankly.

'Doing instead?' I asked. 'What are we doing instead?'

'Why,' said he, 'we are waiting for one or two hours outside this house on a winter evening. You must forgive me; it is all my vanity. It is only to show you that I am right. Can you, with the assistance of this cigar, wait until both Sir Walter Cholmondeliegh and the mystic Wimpole have left this house?'

'Certainly,' I said. 'But I do not know which is likely to leave first. Have you any notion?'

'No,' he said. 'Sir Walter may leave first in a glow of rage. Or again, Mr Wimpole may leave first, feeling that his last epigram is a thing to be flung behind him like a firework. And Sir Walter may remain some time to analyse Mr Wimpole's character. But they will both have to leave within reasonable time, for they will both have to get dressed and come back to dinner here tonight.'

As he spoke the shrill double whistle from the porch of the great house drew a dark cab to the dark portal. And then a thing happened that we really had not expected. Mr Wimpole and Sir Walter Cholmondeliegh came out at the same moment.

They paused for a second or two opposite each other in a natural doubt; then a certain geniality, fundamental perhaps in both of them, made Sir Walter smile and say: 'The night is foggy. Pray take my cab.'

Before I could count twenty the cab had gone rattling up the street with both of them. And before I could count twenty-three Grant had hissed in my ear:

'Run after the cab; run as if you were running from a mad dog – run.'

We pelted on steadily, keeping the cab in sight, through dark mazy streets. God only, I thought, knows why we are running at all, but we are running hard. Fortunately we did not run far. The cab pulled up at the fork of two streets and Sir Walter paid the cabman, who drove away rejoicing, having just come in contact with the more generous among the rich. Then the two men talked together as men do talk together after giving and receiving great insults, the talk that leads either to forgiveness or a duel – at least so it seemed as we watched it from ten yards off. Then the two men shook hands heartily, and one went down one fork of the road and one down another.

Basil, with one of his rare gestures, flung his arms forward.

'Run after that scoundrel,' he cried; 'let us catch him now.'

We dashed across the open space and reached the juncture of two paths.

'Stop!' I shouted wildly to Grant. 'That's the wrong turning.'

He ran on.

'Idiot!' I howled. 'Sir Walter's gone down there. Wimpole has slipped us. He's half a mile down the other road. You're wrong... Are you deaf? You're wrong!'

'I don't think I am,' he panted, and ran on.

'But I saw him!' I cried. 'Look in front of you. Is that Wimpole? It's the old man... What are you doing? What are we to do?'

'Keep running,' said Grant.

Running soon brought us up to the broad back of the pompous old baronet, whose white whiskers shone silver in the fitful lamplight. My brain was utterly bewildered. I grasped nothing.

'Charlie,' said Basil hoarsely, 'can you believe in my common sense for four minutes?'

'Of course,' I said, panting.

'Then help me to catch that man in front and hold him down. Do it at once when I say "Now". Now!'

We sprang on Sir Walter Cholmondeliegh, and rolled that portly old gentleman on his back. He fought with a commendable valour, but we got him tight. I had not the remotest notion why. He had a splendid and full-blooded vigour; when he could not box he kicked, and we bound him; when he could not kick he shouted, and we gagged him. Then, by Basil's arrangement, we dragged him into a small court by the street side and waited. As I say, I had no notion why.

'I am sorry to incommode you,' said Basil calmly out of the darkness; 'but I have made an appointment here.'

'An appointment!' I said blankly.

'Yes,' he said, glancing calmly at the apoplectic old aristocrat gagged on the ground, whose eyes were starting impotently from his head. 'I have made an appointment here with a thoroughly nice young fellow. An old friend. Jasper Drummond his name is – you may have met him this afternoon at the Beaumonts. He can scarcely come though till the Beaumonts' dinner is over.'

For I do not know how many hours we stood there calmly in the darkness. By the time those hours were over I had thoroughly made up my mind that the same thing had happened that had happened long ago on the bench of a British Court of Justice. Basil Grant had gone mad. I could imagine no other explanation of the facts, with the portly, purple-faced old country gentleman flung there strangled on the floor like a bundle of wood.

After about four hours a lean figure in evening dress rushed into the court. A glimpse of gaslight showed the red moustache and white face of Jasper Drummond.

'Mr Grant,' he said blankly, 'the thing is incredible. You were right; but what did you mean? All through this dinner party, where dukes and duchesses and editors of Quarterlies had come especially to hear him, that extraordinary Wimpole kept perfectly silent. He didn't say a funny thing. He didn't say anything at all. What does it mean?'

Grant pointed to the portly old gentleman on the ground.

'That is what it means,' he said.

Drummond, on observing a fat gentleman lying so calmly about the place, jumped back, as from a mouse.

'What?' he said weakly, '... what?'

Basil bent suddenly down and tore a paper out of Sir Walter's breast-pocket, a paper that the baronet, even in his hampered state, seemed to make some effort to retain.

It was a large loose piece of white wrapping paper, which Mr Jasper Drummond read with a vacant eye and undisguised astonishment. As far as he could make out, it consisted of a series of questions and answers, or at least of remarks and replies, arranged in the manner of a catechism. The greater part of the document had been torn and obliterated in the struggle, but the termination remained. It ran as follows:

C. Says... Keep countenance.
W. Keep... British Museum.
C. Know whom talk... absurdities.
W. Never talk absurdities without...

'What is it?' cried Drummond, flinging the paper down in a sort of final fury.

'What is it?' replied Grant, his voice rising into a kind of splendid chant. 'What is it? It is a great new profession. A great new trade. A trifle immoral, I admit, but still great, like piracy.'

'A new profession!' said the young man with the red moustache vaguely; 'a new trade!'

'A new trade,' repeated Grant, with a strange exultation, 'a new profession! What a pity it is immoral.'

'But what the deuce is it?' cried Drummond and I in a breath of blasphemy.

'It is,' said Grant calmly, 'the great new trade of the Organiser of Repartee. This fat old gentleman lying on the ground strikes you, as I have no doubt, as very stupid and very rich. Let me clear his character. He is, like ourselves, very clever and very poor. He is also not really at all fat; all that is stuffing. He is not particularly old, and his name is not Cholmondeliegh. He is a swindler, and a swindler of a perfectly delightful and novel kind. He hires himself out at dinner parties to lead up to other people's repartees. According to a preconcerted scheme (which you may find on that piece of paper), he says the stupid things he has arranged for himself, and his client says the clever things arranged for him. In short, he allows himself to be scored off for a guinea a night.'

'And this fellow Wimpole – ' began Drummond with indignation.

'This fellow Wimpole,' said Basil Grant, smiling, 'will not be an intellectual rival in the future. He had some fine things, elegance and silvered hair, and so on. But the intellect is with our friend on the floor.'

'That fellow,' cried Drummond furiously, 'that fellow ought to be in gaol.'

'Not at all,' said Basil indulgently; 'he ought to be in the Club of Queer Trades.'

3

The Awful Reason of the Vicar's Visit

The revolt of Matter against Man (which I believe to exist) has now been reduced to a singular condition. It is the small things rather than the large things which make war against us and, I may add, beat us. The bones of the last mammoth have long ago decayed, a mighty wreck; the tempests no longer devour our navies, nor the mountains with hearts of fire heap hell over our cities. But we are engaged in a bitter and eternal war with small things; chiefly with microbes and with collar studs. The stud with which I was engaged (on fierce and equal terms) as I made the above reflections, was one that I was trying to introduce into my shirt collar when a loud knock came at the door.

My first thought was as to whether Basil Grant had called to fetch me. He and I were to turn up at the same dinner party (for which I was in the act of dressing), and it might be that he had taken it into his head to come my way, though we had arranged to go separately. It was a small and confidential affair at the table of a good but unconventional political lady, an old friend of his. She had asked us both to meet a third guest, a Captain Fraser, who had made something of a name and was an authority on chimpanzees. As Basil was an old friend of the hostess and I had never seen her, I felt that it was quite possible that he (with his usual social sagacity) might have decided to take me along in order to break the ice. The theory, like all my theories, was complete; but as a fact it was not Basil.

I was handed a visiting card inscribed: 'Rev. Ellis Shorter', and underneath was written in pencil, but in a hand in which even hurry could not conceal a depressing and gentlemanly excellence, 'Asking the favour of a few moments' conversation on a most urgent matter.'

I had already subdued the stud, thereby proclaiming that the image of God has supremacy over all matters (a valuable truth), and throwing on my dress-coat and waistcoat, hurried into the drawing room. He rose at my entrance, flapping like a seal; I can use no other description. He flapped a plaid shawl over his right arm; he flapped a pair of pathetic black gloves; he flapped his clothes; I may say, without exaggeration, that he flapped his eyelids, as he rose. He was a bald-browed, white-haired, white-whiskered old clergyman, of a flappy and floppy type. He said:

'I am so sorry. I am so very sorry. I am so extremely sorry. I come – I can only say – I can only say in my defence, that I come – upon an important matter. Pray forgive me.'

I told him I forgave perfectly and waited.

'What I have to say,' he said brokenly, 'is so dreadful – it is so dreadful – I have lived a quiet life.'

I was burning to get away, for it was already doubtful if I should be in time for dinner. But there was something about the old man's honest air of bitterness that seemed to open to me the possibilities of life larger and more tragic than my own.

I said gently: 'Pray go on.'

Nevertheless the old gentleman, being a gentleman as well as old, noticed my secret impatience and seemed still more unmanned.

'I'm so sorry,' he said meekly; 'I wouldn't have come – but for – your friend Major Brown recommended me to come here.'

'Major Brown!' I said, with some interest.

'Yes,' said the Reverend Mr Shorter, feverishly flapping his plaid shawl about. 'He told me you helped him in a great difficulty – and my difficulty! Oh, my dear sir, it's a matter of life and death.'

I rose abruptly, in an acute perplexity. 'Will it take long, Mr Shorter?' I asked. 'I have to go out to dinner almost at once.'

He rose also, trembling from head to foot, and yet somehow, with all his moral palsy, he rose to the dignity of his age and his office.

'I have no right, Mr Swinburne – I have no right at all,' he said. 'If you have to go out to dinner, you have of course – a perfect right – of course a perfect right. But when you come back – a man will be dead.'

And he sat down, quaking like a jelly.

The triviality of the dinner had been in those two minutes dwarfed and drowned in my mind. I did not want to go and see a political widow, and a captain who collected apes; I wanted to hear what had brought this dear, doddering old vicar into relation with immediate perils.

'Will you have a cigar?' I said.

'No, thank you,' he said, with indescribable embarrassment, as if not smoking cigars was a social disgrace.

'A glass of wine?' I said.

'No, thank you, no, thank you; not just now,' he repeated with that hysterical eagerness with which people who do not drink at all often try to convey that on any other night of the week they would sit up all night drinking rum punch. 'Not just now, thank you.'

'Nothing else I can get for you?' I said, feeling genuinely sorry for the well-mannered old donkey. 'A cup of tea?'

I saw a struggle in his eye and I conquered. When the cup of tea came he drank it like a dipsomaniac gulping brandy. Then he fell back and said:

'I have had such a time, Mr Swinburne. I am not used to these excitements. As Vicar of Chuntsey, in Essex' – he threw this in with an indescribable airiness of vanity – 'I have never known such things happen.'

'What things happen?' I asked.

He straightened himself with sudden dignity.

'As Vicar of Chuntsey, in Essex,' he said, 'I have never been forcibly dressed up as an old woman and made to take part in a crime in the character of an old woman. Never once. My experience may be small. It may be insufficient. But it has never occurred to me before.'

'I have never heard of it,' I said, 'as among the duties of a clergyman. But I am not well up in church matters. Excuse me if perhaps I failed to follow you correctly. Dressed up – as what?'

'As an old woman,' said the vicar solemnly, 'as an old woman.'

I thought in my heart that it required no great transformation to make an old woman of him, but the thing was evidently more tragic than comic, and I said respectfully:

'May I ask how it occurred?'

'I will begin at the beginning,' said Mr Shorter, 'and I will tell my story with the utmost possible precision. At seventeen minutes past eleven this morning I left the vicarage to keep certain appointments and pay certain visits in the village. My first visit was to Mr Jervis, the treasurer of our League of Christian Amusements, with whom I concluded some business touching the claim made by Parkes the gardener in the matter of the rolling of our tennis lawn. I then visited Mrs Arnett, a very earnest churchwoman, but permanently bedridden. She is the author of several small works of devotion, and of a book of verse, entitled (unless my memory misleads me) *Eglantine*.'

He uttered all this not only with deliberation, but with something that can only be called, by a contradictory phrase, eager deliberation. He had, I think, a vague memory in his head of the detectives in the detective stories, who always sternly require that nothing should be kept back.

'I then proceeded,' he went on, with the same maddening conscientiousness of manner, 'to Mr Carr (not Mr James Carr, of course; Mr Robert Carr) who is temporarily assisting our organist, and having consulted with him (on the subject of a choir boy who is accused, I cannot as yet say whether justly or not, of cutting holes in the organ pipes), I finally dropped in upon a Dorcas meeting at the house of Miss Brett. The Dorcas meetings are usually held at the vicarage, but my wife being unwell, Miss Brett, a newcomer in our village, but very active in church work, had very kindly consented to hold them. The Dorcas society is entirely under my wife's management as a rule, and except for Miss Brett, who, as I say, is very active, I scarcely know any members of it. I had, however, promised to drop in on them, and I did so.

'When I arrived there were only four other maiden ladies with Miss Brett, but they were sewing very busily. It is very difficult, of course, for any person, however strongly impressed with the necessity in these matters of full and exact exposition of the facts, to remember and repeat the actual details of a conversation, particularly a conversation that (though inspired with a most worthy and admirable zeal for good work) was one which did not greatly impress the hearer's mind at the time and was in fact – er – mostly about socks. I can, however, remember distinctly that one of the spinster ladies (she was a thin person with a woollen shawl, who appeared to feel the cold, and I am almost sure she was introduced to me as Miss James) remarked that the weather was very changeable. Miss Brett then offered me a cup of tea, which I accepted, I cannot recall in what words. Miss Brett is a short and stout lady with white hair. The only other figure in the group that caught my attention was a Miss Mowbray, a small and neat lady of aristocratic manners, silver hair, and a high voice and colour. She was the most emphatic member of the party; and her views on the subject of pinafores, though expressed with a natural deference to myself, were in themselves strong and advanced. Beside her (although all five ladies were dressed simply in black) it could not be denied that the others looked in some way what you men of the world would call dowdy.

'After about ten minutes' conversation I rose to go, and as I did so I heard something that – I cannot describe it – something that seemed to – but I really cannot describe it.'

'What did you hear?' I asked, with some impatience.

'I heard,' said the vicar solemnly, 'I heard Miss Mowbray (the lady with the silver hair) say to Miss James (the lady with the woollen shawl), the following extraordinary words. I committed them to memory on the spot, and as soon as circumstances set me free to do so, I noted them down on a piece of paper. I believe I have it here.' He fumbled in his breast-pocket, bringing out mild things, notebooks, circulars and programmes of village concerts. 'I heard Miss Mowbray say to Miss James, the following words: "Now's your time, Bill."'

He gazed at me for a few moments after making this announcement, gravely and unflinchingly, as if conscious that here he was unshaken about his facts. Then he resumed, turning his bald head more towards the fire.

'This appeared to me remarkable. I could not by any means understand it. It seemed to me first of all peculiar that one maiden lady should address another maiden lady as "Bill". My experience, as I have said, may be incomplete; maiden ladies may have among themselves and in exclusively spinster circles wilder customs than I am aware of. But it seemed to me odd, and I could almost have sworn (if you will not misunderstand the phrase), I should have been strongly impelled to maintain at the time that the words, "Now's your time, Bill", were by no means pronounced with that upper-class intonation which, as I have already said, had up to now characterised Miss Mowbray's conversation. In fact, the words, "Now's your time, Bill", would have been, I fancy, unsuitable if pronounced with that upper-class intonation.

'I was surprised, I repeat, then, at the remark. But I was still more surprised when, looking round me in bewilderment, my hat and umbrella in hand, I saw the lean lady with the woollen shawl leaning upright against the door out of which I was just about to make my exit. She was still knitting, and I supposed that this erect posture against the door was only an eccentricity of spinsterhood and an oblivion of my intended departure.

'I said genially, "I am so sorry to disturb you, Miss James, but I must really be going. I have – er – " I stopped here, for the words she had uttered in reply, though singularly brief and in tone extremely businesslike, were such as to render that arrest of my remarks, I think, natural and excusable. I have these words also noted down. I have not the least idea of their meaning; so I have only been able to render them phonetically. But she said,' and Mr Shorter peered short-sightedly at his papers, 'she said: "Chuck it, fat 'ead," and she added something that sounded like "It's a kop", or (possibly) "a kopt". And then the last cord, either of my sanity or the sanity of the universe, snapped suddenly. My esteemed friend and helper, Miss Brett, standing by the mantelpiece, said: "Put 'is old 'ead in a bag, Sam, and tie 'im up before you start jawin'. You'll be kopt yourselves some o' these days with this way of doin' things, har lar theater.'

'My head went round and round. Was it really true, as I had suddenly fancied a moment before, that unmarried ladies had some dreadful riotous society of their own from which all others were excluded? I remembered dimly in my classical days (I was a scholar in a small way once, but now, alas! rusty), I remembered the mysteries of the Bona Dea[13] and their strange female freemasonry. I remembered the witches' Sabbaths. I was just, in my absurd lightheadedness, trying to remember a line of verse about Diana's nymphs, when Miss Mowbray threw her arm round me from behind. The moment it held me I knew it was not a woman's arm.

'Miss Brett – or what I had called Miss Brett – was standing in front of me with a big revolver in her hand and a broad grin on her face. Miss James was still leaning against the door, but had fallen into an attitude so totally new, and so totally unfeminine, that it gave one a shock. She was kicking her heels, with her hands in her pockets and her cap on one side. She was a man. I mean he was a wo – no, that is I saw that instead of being a woman she – he, I mean – that is, it was a man.'

Mr Shorter became indescribably flurried and flapping in endeavouring to arrange these genders and his plaid shawl at the same time. He resumed with a higher fever of nervousness:

'As for Miss Mowbray, she – he, held me in a ring of iron. He had her arm – that is she had his arm – round her neck – my neck I mean – and I could not cry out. Miss Brett – that is, Mr Brett, at least Mr something who was not Miss Brett – had the revolver pointed at me. The other two ladies – or er – gentlemen, were rummaging in some bag in the background. It was all clear at last: they were criminals dressed up as women, to kidnap me! To kidnap the Vicar of Chuntsey, in Essex. But why? Was it to be Nonconformists?

'The brute leaning against the door called out carelessly, "'Urry up, 'Arry. Show the old bloke what the game is, and let's get off."

'"Curse 'is eyes," said Miss Brett – I mean the man with the revolver – "why should we show 'im the game?"

'"If you take my advice you bloomin' well will," said the man at the door, whom they called Bill. "A man wot knows wot 'e's doin' is worth ten wot don't, even if 'e's a potty old parson."

'"Bill's right enough," said the coarse voice of the man who held me (it had been Miss Mowbray's). "Bring out the picture, 'Arry."

'The man with the revolver walked across the room to where the other two women – I mean men – were turning over baggage, and asked them for something which they gave him. He came back with it across the room and held it out in front of me. And compared to the surprise of that display, all the previous surprises of this awful day shrank suddenly.

'It was a portrait of myself. That such a picture should be in the hands of these scoundrels might in any case have caused a mild surprise; but no more. It was no mild surprise that I felt. The likeness was an extremely good one, worked up with all the accessories of the conventional photographic studio. I was leaning my head on my hand and was relieved against a painted landscape of woodland. It was obvious that it was no snapshot; it was clear that I had sat for this photograph. And the truth was that I had never sat for such a photograph. It was a photograph that I had never had taken.

'I stared at it again and again. It seemed to me to be touched up a good deal; it was glazed as well as framed, and the glass blurred some of the details. But there unmistakably was my face, my eyes, my nose and mouth, my head and hand, posed for a professional photographer. And I had never posed so for any photographer.

'"Be'old the bloomin' miracle," said the man with the revolver, with ill-timed facetiousness. "Parson, prepare to meet your God." And with this he slid the glass out of the frame. As the glass moved, I saw that part of the picture was painted on it in Chinese white, notably a pair of white whiskers and a clerical collar. And underneath was a portrait of an old lady in a quiet black dress, leaning her head on her hand against the woodland landscape. The old lady was as like me as one pin is like another. It had required only the whiskers and the collar to make it me in every hair.

'"Entertainin', ain't it?" said the man described as 'Arry, as he shot the glass back again. "Remarkable resemblance, parson. Gratifyin' to the lady. Gratifyin' to you. And hi may hadd, particlery gratifyin' to us, as bein' the probable source of a very tolerable haul. You know Colonel Hawker, the man who's come to live in these parts, don't you?"

'I nodded.

'"Well," said the man 'Arry, pointing to the picture, "that's 'is mother. 'Oo ran to catch 'im when 'e fell? She did," and he flung his fingers in a general gesture towards the photograph of the old lady who was exactly like me.

'"Tell the old gent wot 'e's got to do and be done with it," broke out Bill from the door. "Look 'ere, Reverend Shorter, we ain't goin' to do you no 'arm. We'll give you a sov. for your trouble if you like. And as for the old woman's clothes – why, you'll look lovely in 'em."

'"You ain't much of a 'and at a description, Bill,' said the man behind me. "Mr Shorter, it's like this. We've got to see this man Hawker tonight. Maybe 'e'll kiss us all and 'ave up the champagne when 'e sees us. Maybe on the other 'and – 'e won't. Maybe 'e'll be dead when we goes away. Maybe not. But we've got to see 'im. Now as you know, 'e shuts 'isself up and never opens the door to a soul; only you don't know why and we does. The only one as can ever get at 'im is 'is mother. Well, it's a confounded funny coincidence," he said, accenting the penultimate, "it's a very unusual piece of good luck, but you're 'is mother."

'"When first I saw 'er picture," said the man Bill, shaking his head in a ruminant manner, "when I first saw it I said – old Shorter. Those were my exact words – old Shorter."

'"What do you mean, you wild creatures?" I gasped. "What am I to do?"

'"That's easy said, your 'oldness," said the man with the revolver, good-humouredly; "you've got to put on those clothes," and he pointed to a poke bonnet[14] and a heap of female clothes in the corner of the room.

'I will not dwell, Mr Swinburne, upon the details of what followed. I had no choice. I could not fight five men, to say nothing of a loaded pistol. In five minutes, sir, the Vicar of Chuntsey was dressed as an old woman – as somebody else's mother, if you please – and was dragged out of the house to take part in a crime.

'It was already late in the afternoon, and the nights of winter were closing in fast. On a dark road, in a blowing wind, we set out towards the lonely house of Colonel Hawker, perhaps the queerest cortege that ever straggled up that or any other road. To every human eye, in every external, we were six very respectable old ladies of small means, in black dresses and refined but antiquated bonnets; and we were really five criminals and a clergyman.

'I will cut a long story short. My brain was whirling like a windmill as I walked, trying to think of some manner of escape. To cry out, so long as we were far from houses, would be suicidal, for it would be easy for the ruffians to knife me or to gag me and fling me into a ditch. On the other hand, to attempt to stop strangers and explain the situation was impossible, because of the frantic folly of the situation itself. Long before I had persuaded the chance postman or carrier of so absurd a story, my companions would certainly have got off themselves, and in all probability would have carried me off, as a friend of theirs who had the misfortune to be mad or drunk. The last thought, however, was an inspiration; though a very terrible one. Had it come to this, that the Vicar of Chuntsey must pretend to be mad or drunk? It had come to this.

'I walked along with the rest up the deserted road, imitating and keeping pace, as far as I could, with their rapid and yet ladylike step, until at length I saw a lamppost and a policeman standing under it. I had made up my mind. Until we reached them we were all equally demure and silent and swift. When we reached them I suddenly flung myself against the railings and roared out: "Hooray! Hooray! Hooray! Rule Britannia! Get your 'air cut. Hoop-la! Boo!" It was a condition of no little novelty for a man in my position.

'The constable instantly flashed his lantern on me, or the draggled, drunken old woman that was my travesty. "Now then, mum," he began gruffly.

'"Come along quiet, or I'll eat your heart," cried Sam in my ear hoarsely. "Stop, or I'll flay you." It was frightful to hear the words and see the neatly shawled old spinster who whispered them.

'I yelled, and yelled – I was in for it now. I screamed comic refrains that vulgar young men had sung, to my regret, at our village concerts; I rolled to and fro like a ninepin about to fall.

'"If you can't get your friend on quiet, ladies," said the policeman, "I shall have to take 'er up. Drunk and disorderly she is right enough."

'I redoubled my efforts. I had not been brought up to this sort of thing; but I believe I eclipsed myself. Words that I did not know I had ever heard of seemed to come pouring out of my open mouth.

'"When we get you past," whispered Bill, "you'll howl louder; you'll howl louder when we're burning your feet off."

'I screamed in my terror those awful songs of joy. In all the nightmares that men have ever dreamed, there has never been anything so blighting and horrible as the faces of those five men, looking out of their poke bonnets; the figures of district visitors with the faces of devils. I cannot think there is anything so heartbreaking in hell.

'For a sickening instant I thought that the bustle of my companions and the perfect respectability of all our dresses would overcome the policeman and induce him to let us pass. He wavered, so far as one can describe anything so solid as a policeman as wavering. I lurched suddenly forward and ran my head into his chest, calling out (if I remember correctly), "Oh, crikey, blimey, Bill." It was at that moment that I remembered most dearly that I was the Vicar of Chuntsey, in Essex.

'My desperate coup saved me. The policeman had me hard by the back of the neck.

'"You come along with me," he began, but Bill cut in with his perfect imitation of a lady's finnicking voice.

'"Oh, pray, constable, don't make a disturbance with our poor friend. We will get her quietly home. She does drink too much, but she is quite a lady – only eccentric."

'"She butted me in the stomach," said the policeman briefly.

'"Eccentricities of genius," said Sam earnestly.

'"Pray let me take her home," reiterated Bill, in the resumed character of Miss James, "she wants looking after."

'"She does," said the policeman, "but I'll look after her."

'"That's no good," cried Bill feverishly. "She wants her friends. She wants a particular medicine we've got."

'"Yes," assented Miss Mowbray, with excitement, "no other medicine any good, constable. Complaint quite unique."

'"I'm all righ'. Cutchy, cutchy, coo!" remarked, to his eternal shame, the Vicar of Chuntsey.

'"Look here, ladies," said the constable sternly, "I don't like the eccentricity of your friend, and I don't like 'er songs, or 'er 'ead in my stomach. And now I come to think of it, I don't like the looks of you. I've seen many as quiet dressed as you as was wrong 'uns. Who are you?"

'"We've not our cards with us," said Miss Mowbray, with indescribable dignity. "Nor do we see why we should be insulted by any Jack-in-office who chooses to be rude to ladies, when he is paid to protect them. If you choose to take advantage of the weakness of our unfortunate friend, no doubt you are legally entitled to take her. But if you fancy you have any legal right to bully us, you will find yourself in the wrong box."

'The truth and dignity of this staggered the policeman for a moment. Under cover of their advantage my five persecutors turned for an instant on me faces like faces of the damned and then swished off into the darkness. When the constable first turned his lantern and his suspicions on to them, I had seen the telegraphic look flash from face to face saying that only retreat was possible now.

'By this time I was sinking slowly to the pavement, in a state of acute reflection. So long as the ruffians were with me, I dared not quit the role of drunkard. For if I had begun to talk reasonably and explain the real case, the officer would merely have thought that I was slightly recovered and would have put me in charge of my friends. Now, however, if I liked I might safely undeceive him.

'But I confess I did not like. The chances of life are many, and it may doubtless sometimes lie in the narrow path of duty for a clergyman of the Church of England to pretend to be a drunken old woman; but such necessities are, I imagine, sufficiently rare to appear to many improbable. Suppose the story got about that I had pretended to be drunk. Suppose people did not all think it was pretence!

'I lurched up, the policeman half-lifting me. I went along weakly and quietly for about a hundred yards. The officer evidently thought that I was too sleepy and feeble to effect an escape, and so held me lightly and easily enough. Past one turning, two turnings, three turnings, four turnings, he trailed me with him, a limp and slow and reluctant figure. At the fourth turning, I suddenly broke from his hand and tore down the street like a maddened stag. He was unprepared, he was heavy, and it was dark. I ran and ran and ran, and in five minutes' running, found I was gaining. In half an hour I was out in the fields under the holy and blessed stars, where I tore off my accursed shawl and bonnet and buried them in clean earth.'

The old gentleman had finished his story and leant back in his chair. Both the matter and the manner of his narration had, as time went on, impressed me favourably. He was an old duffer and pedant, but behind these things he was a country-bred man and gentleman, and had showed courage and a sporting instinct in the hour of desperation. He had told his story with many quaint formalities of diction, but also with a very convincing realism.

'And now – ' I began.

'And now,' said Shorter, leaning forward again with something like servile energy, 'and now, Mr Swinburne, what about that unhappy man Hawker. I cannot tell what those men meant, or how far what they said was real. But surely there is danger. I cannot go to the police, for reasons that you perceive. Among other things, they wouldn't believe me. What is to be done?'

I took out my watch. It was already half-past twelve.

'My friend Basil Grant,' I said, 'is the best man we can go to. He and I were to have gone to the same dinner tonight; but he will just have come back by now. Have you any objection to taking a cab?'

'Not at all,' he replied, rising politely, and gathering up his absurd plaid shawl.

A rattle in a hansom brought us underneath the sombre pile of workmen's flats in Lambeth which Grant inhabited; a climb up a wearisome wooden staircase brought us to his garret. When I entered that wooden and scrappy interior, the white gleam of Basil's shirt front and the lustre of his fur coat flung on the wooden settle, struck me as a contrast. He was drinking a glass of wine before retiring. I was right; he had come back from the dinner party.

He listened to the repetition of the story of the Rev. Ellis Shorter with the genuine simplicity and respect which he never failed to exhibit in dealing with any human being. When it was over he said simply:

'Do you know a man named Captain Fraser?'

I was so startled at this totally irrelevant reference to the worthy collector of chimpanzees with whom I ought to have dined that evening, that I glanced sharply at Grant. The result was that I did not look at Mr Shorter. I only heard him answer, in his most nervous tone, 'No.'

Basil, however, seemed to find something very curious about his answer or his demeanour generally, for he kept his big blue eyes fixed on the old clergyman, and though the eyes were quite quiet they stood out more and more from his head.

'You are quite sure, Mr Shorter,' he repeated, 'that you don't know Captain Fraser?'

'Quite,' answered the vicar, and I was certainly puzzled to find him returning so much to the timidity, not to say the demoralisation, of his tone when he first entered my presence.

Basil sprang smartly to his feet.

'Then our course is clear,' he said. 'You have not even begun your investigation, my dear Mr Shorter; the first thing for us to do is to go together to see Captain Fraser.'

'When?' asked the clergyman, stammering.

'Now,' said Basil, putting one arm in his fur coat.

The old clergyman rose to his feet, quaking all over.

'I really do not think that it is necessary,' he said.

Basil took his arm out of the fur coat, threw it over the chair again, and put his hands in his pockets.

'Oh,' he said, with emphasis. 'Oh – you don't think it necessary; then,' and he added the words with great clearness and deliberation, 'then, Mr Ellis Shorter, I can only say that I would like to see you without your whiskers.'

And at these words I also rose to my feet, for the great tragedy of my life had come. Splendid and exciting as life was in continual contact with an intellect like Basil's, I had always the feeling that that splendour and excitement were on the borderland of sanity. He lived perpetually near the vision of the reason of things which makes men lose their reason. And I felt of his insanity as men feel of the death of friends with heart disease. It might come anywhere, in a field, in a hansom cab, looking at a sunset, smoking a cigarette. It had come now. At the very moment of delivering a judgement for the salvation of a fellow creature, Basil Grant had gone mad.

'Your whiskers,' he cried, advancing with blazing eyes. 'Give me your whiskers. And your bald head.'

The old vicar naturally retreated a step or two. I stepped between.

'Sit down, Basil,' I implored, 'you're a little excited. Finish your wine.'

'Whiskers,' he answered sternly, 'whiskers.'

And with that he made a dash at the old gentleman, who made a dash for the door, but was intercepted. And then, before I knew where I was the quiet room was turned into something between a pantomime and a pandemonium by those two. Chairs were flung over with a crash, tables were vaulted with a noise like thunder, screens were smashed, crockery scattered in smithereens, and still Basil Grant bounded and bellowed after the Rev. Ellis Shorter.

And now I began to perceive something else, which added the last half-witted touch to my mystification. The Rev. Ellis Shorter, of Chuntsey, in Essex, was by no means behaving as I had previously noticed him to behave, or as, considering his age and station, I should have expected him to behave. His power of dodging, leaping and fighting would have been amazing in a lad of seventeen, and in this doddering old vicar looked like a sort of farcical fairy tale. Moreover, he did not seem to be so much astonished as I had thought. There was even a look of something like enjoyment in his eyes; so there was in the eye of Basil. In fact, the unintelligible truth must be told. They were both laughing.

At length Shorter was cornered.

'Come, come, Mr Grant,' he panted, 'you can't do anything to me. It's quite legal. And it doesn't do any one the least harm. It's only a social fiction. A result of our complex society, Mr Grant.'

'I don't blame you, my man,' said Basil coolly. 'But I want your whiskers. And your bald head. Do they belong to Captain Fraser?'

'No, no,' said Mr Shorter, laughing, 'we provide them ourselves. They don't belong to Captain Fraser.'

'What the deuce does all this mean?' I almost screamed. 'Are you all in an infernal nightmare? Why should Mr Shorter's bald head belong to Captain Fraser? How could it? What the deuce has Captain Fraser to do with the affair? What is the matter with him? You dined with him, Basil.'

'No,' said Grant, 'I didn't.'

'Didn't you go to Mrs Thornton's dinner party?' I asked, staring. 'Why not?'

'Well,' said Basil, with a slow and singular smile, 'the fact is I was detained by a visitor. I have him, as a point of fact, in my bedroom.'

'In your bedroom?' I repeated; but my imagination had reached that point when he might have said in his coal scuttle or his waistcoat pocket.

Grant stepped to the door of an inner room, flung it open and walked in. Then he came out again with the last of the bodily wonders of that wild night. He introduced into the sitting room, in an apologetic manner, and by the nape of the neck, a limp clergyman with a bald head, white whiskers and a plaid shawl.

'Sit down, gentlemen,' cried Grant, striking his hands heartily. 'Sit down all of you and have a glass of wine. As you say, there is no harm in it, and if Captain Fraser had simply dropped me a hint I could have saved him from dropping a good sum of money. Not that you would have liked that, eh?'

The two duplicate clergymen, who were sipping their Burgundy with two duplicate grins, laughed heartily at this, and one of them carelessly pulled off his whiskers and laid them on the table.

'Basil,' I said, 'if you are my friend, save me. What is all this?'

He laughed again.

'Only another addition, Cherub, to your collection of Queer Trades. These two gentlemen (whose health I have now the pleasure of drinking) are Professional Detainers.'

'And what on earth's that?' I asked.

'It's really very simple, Mr Swinburne,' began he who had once been the Rev. Ellis Shorter, of Chuntsey, in Essex; and it gave me a shock indescribable to hear out of that pompous and familiar form come no longer its own pompous and familiar voice, but the brisk sharp tones of a young city man. 'It is really nothing very important. We are paid by our clients to detain in conversation, on some harmless pretext, people whom they want out of the way for a few hours. And Captain Fraser – ' and with that he hesitated and smiled.

Basil smiled also. He intervened.

'The fact is that Captain Fraser, who is one of my best friends, wanted us both out of the way very much. He is sailing tonight for East Africa, and the lady with whom we were all to have dined is – er – what is I believe described as "the romance of his life". He wanted that two hours with her, and employed these two reverend gentlemen to detain us at our houses so as to let him have the field to himself.'

'And of course,' said the late Mr Shorter apologetically to me, 'as I had to keep a gentleman at home from keeping an appointment with a lady, I had to come with something rather hot and strong – rather urgent. It wouldn't have done to be tame.'

'Oh,' I said, 'I acquit you of tameness.'

'Thank you, sir,' said the man respectfully, 'always very grateful for any recommendation, sir.'

The other man idly pushed back his artificial bald head, revealing close red hair, and spoke dreamily, perhaps under the influence of Basil's admirable Burgundy.

'It's wonderful how common it's getting, gentlemen. Our office is busy from morning till night. I've no doubt you've often knocked up against us before. You just take notice. When an old bachelor goes on boring you with hunting stories, when you're burning to be introduced to somebody, he's from our bureau. When a lady calls on parish work and stops hours, just when you wanted to go to the Robinsons', she's from our bureau. The Robinson hand, sir, may be darkly seen.'

'There is one thing I don't understand,' I said. 'Why you are both vicars.'

A shade crossed the brow of the temporary incumbent of Chuntsey, in Essex.

'That may have been a mistake, sir,' he said. 'But it was not our fault. It was all the munificence of Captain Fraser. He requested that the highest price and talent on our tariff should be employed to detain you gentlemen. Now the highest payment in our office goes to those who impersonate vicars, as being the most respectable and more of a strain. We are paid five guineas a visit. We have had the good fortune to satisfy the firm with our work; and we are now permanently vicars. Before that we had two years as colonels, the next in our scale. Colonels are four guineas.'

4

The Singular Speculation of the House-Agent

Lieutenant Drummond Keith was a man about whom conversation always burst like a thunderstorm the moment he left the room. This arose from many separate touches about him. He was a light, loose person, who wore light, loose clothes, generally white, as if he were in the tropics; he was lean and graceful, like a panther, and he had restless black eyes.

He was very impecunious. He had one of the habits of the poor, in a degree so exaggerated as immeasurably to eclipse the most miserable of the unemployed; I mean the habit of continual change of lodgings. There are inland tracts of London where, in the very heart of artificial civilisation, humanity has almost become nomadic once more. But in that restless interior there was no ragged tramp so restless as the elegant officer in the loose white clothes. He had shot a great many things in his time, to judge from his conversation, from partridges to elephants, but his slangier acquaintances were of opinion that 'the moon' had been not unfrequently amid the victims of his victorious rifle. The phrase is a fine one, and suggests a mystic, elvish, nocturnal hunting.

He carried from house to house and from parish to parish a kit which consisted practically of five articles. Two odd-looking, large-bladed spears, tied together, the weapons, I suppose, of some savage tribe, a green umbrella, a huge and tattered copy of *The Pickwick Papers*, a big game rifle, and a large sealed jar of some unholy oriental wine. These always went into every new lodging, even for one night; and they went in quite undisguised, tied up in wisps of string or straw, to the delight of the poetic gutter boys in the little grey streets.

I had forgotten to mention that he always carried also his old regimental sword. But this raised another odd question about him. Slim and active as he was, he was no longer very young. His hair, indeed, was quite grey, though his rather wild almost Italian moustache retained its blackness, and his face was care-worn under its almost Italian gaiety. To find a middle-aged man who has left the Army at the primitive rank of lieutenant is unusual and not necessarily encouraging. With the more cautious and solid this fact, like his endless flitting, did the mysterious gentleman no good.

Lastly, he was a man who told the kind of adventures which win a man admiration, but not respect. They came out of queer places, where a good man would scarcely find himself, out of opium dens and gambling hells; they had the heat of the thieves' kitchens or smelled of a strange smoke from cannibal incantations. These are the kind of stories which discredit a person almost equally whether they are believed or no. If Keith's tales were false he was a liar; if they were true he had had, at any rate, every opportunity of being a scamp.

He had just left the room in which I sat with Basil Grant and his brother Rupert, the voluble amateur detective. And as I say was invariably the case, we were all talking about him. Rupert Grant was a clever young fellow, but he had that tendency that youth and cleverness, when sharply combined, so often produce, a somewhat extravagant scepticism. He saw doubt and guilt everywhere, and it was meat and drink to him. I had often got irritated with this boyish incredulity of his, but on this particular occasion I am bound to say that I thought him so obviously right that I was astounded at Basil's opposing him, however banteringly.

I could swallow a good deal, being naturally of a simple turn, but I could not swallow Lieutenant Keith's autobiography.

'You don't seriously mean, Basil,' I said, 'that you think that that fellow really did go as a stowaway with Nansen[15] and pretend to be the Mad Mullah[16] and – '

'He has one fault,' said Basil thoughtfully, 'or virtue, as you may happen to regard it. He tells the truth in too exact and bald a style; he is too veracious.'

'Oh! if you are going to be paradoxical,' said Rupert contemptuously, 'be a bit funnier than that. Say, for instance, that he has lived all his life in one ancestral manor.'

'No, he's extremely fond of change of scene,' replied Basil dispassionately, 'and of living in odd places. That doesn't prevent his chief trait being verbal exactitude. What you people don't understand is that telling a thing crudely and coarsely as it happened makes it sound frightfully strange. The sort of things Keith recounts are not the sort of things that a man would make up to cover himself with honour; they are too absurd. But they are the sort of things that a man would do if he were sufficiently filled with the soul of skylarking.'

'So far from paradox,' said his brother, with something rather like a sneer, 'you seem to be going in for journalese proverbs. Do you believe that truth is stranger than fiction?'

'Truth must of necessity be stranger than fiction,' said Basil placidly. 'For fiction is the creation of the human mind, and therefore is congenial to it.'

'Well, your lieutenant's truth is stranger, if it is truth, than anything I ever heard of,' said Rupert, relapsing into flippancy. 'Do you, on your soul, believe in all that about the shark and the camera?'

'I believe Keith's words,' answered the other. 'He is an honest man.'

'I should like to question a regiment of his landladies,' said Rupert cynically.

'I must say, I think you can hardly regard him as unimpeach-able merely in himself,' I said mildly; 'his mode of life – '

Before I could complete the sentence the door was flung open and Drummond Keith appeared again on the threshold, his white Panama on his head.

'I say, Grant,' he said, knocking off his cigarette ash against the door, 'I've got no money in the world till next April. Could you lend me a hundred pounds? There's a good chap.'

Rupert and I looked at each other in an ironical silence. Basil, who was sitting by his desk, swung the chair round idly on its screw and picked up a quill pen.

'Shall I cross it?' he asked, opening a cheque-book.

'Really,' began Rupert, with a rather nervous loudness, 'since Lieutenant Keith has seen fit to make this suggestion to Basil before his family, I – '

'Here you are, Ugly,' said Basil, fluttering a cheque in the direction of the quite nonchalant officer. 'Are you in a hurry?'

'Yes,' replied Keith, in a rather abrupt way. 'As a matter of fact I want it now. I want to see my – er – businessman.'

Rupert was eyeing him sarcastically, and I could see that it was on the tip of his tongue to say, enquiringly, 'Receiver of stolen goods, perhaps.' What he did say was:

'A businessman? That's rather a general description, Lieutenant Keith.'

Keith looked at him sharply, and then said, with something rather like ill-temper:

'He's a thingumabob, a house-agent, say. I'm going to see him.'

'Oh, you're going to see a house-agent, are you?' said Rupert Grant grimly. 'Do you know, Mr Keith, I think I should very much like to go with you?'

Basil shook with his soundless laughter. Lieutenant Keith started a little; his brow blackened sharply.

'I beg your pardon,' he said. 'What did you say?'

Rupert's face had been growing from stage to stage of ferocious irony, and he answered:

'I was saying that I wondered whether you would mind our strolling along with you to this house-agent's.'

The visitor swung his stick with a sudden whirling violence.

'Oh, in God's name, come to my house-agent's! Come to my bedroom. Look under my bed. Examine my dustbin. Come along!' And with a furious energy that took away our breath he banged his way out of the room.

Rupert Grant, his restless blue eyes dancing with his detective excitement, soon shouldered alongside him, talking to him with that transparent camaraderie that he imagined to be appropriate from the disguised policeman to the disguised criminal. His interpretation was certainly corroborated by one particular detail, the unmistakable unrest, annoyance and nervousness of the man with whom he walked. Basil and I tramped behind, and it was not necessary for us to tell each other that we had both noticed this.

Lieutenant Drummond Keith led us through very extraordinary and unpromising neighbourhoods in the search for his remarkable house-agent. Neither of the brothers Grant failed to notice this fact. As the streets grew closer and more crooked and the roofs lower and the gutters grosser with mud, a darker curiosity deepened on the brows of Basil, and the figure of Rupert seen from behind seemed to fill the street with a gigantic swagger of success. At length, at the end of the fourth or fifth lean grey street in that sterile district, we came suddenly to a halt, the mysterious lieutenant looking once more about him with a sort of sulky desperation. Above a row of shutters and a door, all indescribably dingy in appearance and in size scarce sufficient even for a penny toyshop, ran the inscription: 'P. Montmorency, House-Agent.'

'This is the office of which I spoke,' said Keith, in a cutting voice. 'Will you wait here a moment, or does your astonishing tenderness about my welfare lead you to wish to overhear everything I have to say to my business adviser?'

Rupert's face was white and shaking with excitement; nothing on earth would have induced him now to have abandoned his prey.

'If you will excuse me,' he said, clenching his hands behind his back, 'I think I should feel myself justified in – '

'Oh! Come along in,' exploded the lieutenant. He made the same gesture of savage surrender. And he slammed into the office, the rest of us at his heels.

P. Montmorency, House-Agent, was a solitary old gentleman sitting behind a bare brown counter. He had an egglike head, froglike jaws, and a grey hairy fringe of aureole round the lower part of his face; the whole combined with a reddish, aquiline nose. He wore a shabby black frock-coat, a sort of semi-clerical tie worn at a very unclerical angle, and looked, generally speaking, about as unlike a house-agent as anything could look, short of something like a sandwich man or a Scotch Highlander.

We stood inside the room for fully forty seconds, and the odd old gentleman did not look at us. Neither, to tell the truth, odd as he was, did we look at him. Our eyes were fixed, where his were fixed, upon something that was crawling about on the counter in front of him. It was a ferret.

The silence was broken by Rupert Grant. He spoke in that sweet and steely voice which he reserved for great occasions and practised for hours together in his bedroom. He said:

'Mr Montmorency, I think?'

The old gentleman started, lifted his eyes with a bland bewilderment, picked up the ferret by the neck, stuffed it alive into his trousers pocket, smiled apologetically, and said:

'Sir.'

'You are a house-agent, are you not?' asked Rupert.

To the delight of that criminal investigator, Mr Montmorency's eyes wandered unquietly towards Lieutenant Keith, the only man present that he knew.

'A house-agent,' cried Rupert again, bringing out the word as if it were 'burglar'.

'Yes... oh, yes,' said the man, with a quavering and almost coquettish smile. 'I am a house-agent... oh, yes.'

'Well, I think,' said Rupert, with a sardonic sleekness, 'that Lieutenant Keith wants to speak to you. We have come in by his request.'

Lieutenant Keith was lowering gloomily, and now he spoke.

'I have come, Mr Montmorency, about that house of mine.'

'Yes, sir,' said Montmorency, spreading his fingers on the flat counter. 'It's all ready, sir. I've attended to all your suggestions er – about the br – '

'Right,' cried Keith, cutting the word short with the startling neatness of a gunshot. 'We needn't bother about all that. If you've done what I told you, all right.'

And he turned sharply towards the door.

Mr Montmorency, House-Agent, presented a picture of pathos. After stammering a moment he said: 'Excuse me... Mr Keith... there was another matter... about which I wasn't quite sure. I tried to get all the heating apparatus possible under the circumstances... but in winter... at that elevation...'

'Can't expect much, eh?' said the lieutenant, cutting in with the same sudden skill. 'No, of course not. That's all right, Montmorency. There can't be any more difficulties,' and he put his hand on the handle of the door.

'I think,' said Rupert Grant, with a satanic suavity, 'that Mr Montmorency has something further to say to you, lieutenant.'

'Only,' said the house-agent, in desperation, 'what about the birds?'

'I beg your pardon,' said Rupert, in a general blank.

'What about the birds?' said the house-agent doggedly.

Basil, who had remained throughout the proceedings in a state of Napoleonic calm, which might be more accurately described as a state of Napoleonic stupidity, suddenly lifted his leonine head.

'Before you go, Lieutenant Keith,' he said. 'Come now. Really, what about the birds?'

'I'll take care of them,' said Lieutenant Keith, still with his long back turned to us; 'they shan't suffer.'

'Thank you, sir, thank you,' cried the incomprehensible house-agent, with an air of ecstasy. 'You'll excuse my concern, sir. You know I'm wild on wild animals. I'm as wild as any of them on that. Thank you, sir. But there's another thing...'

The lieutenant, with his back turned to us, exploded with an indescribable laugh and swung round to face us. It was a laugh, the purport of which was direct and essential, and yet which one cannot exactly express. As near as it said anything, verbally speaking, it said: 'Well, if you must spoil it, you must. But you don't know what you're spoiling.'

'There is another thing,' continued Mr Montmorency weakly. 'Of course, if you don't want to be visited you'll paint the house green, but – '

'Green!' shouted Keith. 'Green! Let it be green or nothing. I won't have a house of another colour. Green!' and before we could realise anything the door had banged between us and the street.

Rupert Grant seemed to take a little time to collect himself; but he spoke before the echoes of the door died away.

'Your client, Lieutenant Keith, appears somewhat excited,' he said. 'What is the matter with him? Is he unwell?'

'Oh, I should think not,' said Mr Montmorency, in some confusion. 'The negotiations have been somewhat difficult – the house is rather – '

'Green,' said Rupert calmly. 'That appears to be a very important point. It must be rather green. May I ask you, Mr Montmorency, before I rejoin my companion outside, whether, in your business, it is usual to ask for houses by their colour? Do clients write to a house-agent asking for a pink house or a blue house? Or, to take another instance, for a green house?'

'Only,' said Montmorency, trembling, 'only to be inconspicuous.'

Rupert had his ruthless smile. 'Can you tell me any place on earth in which a green house would be inconspicuous?'

The house-agent was fidgeting nervously in his pocket. Slowly drawing out a couple of lizards and leaving them to run on the counter, he said:

'No; I can't.'

'You can't suggest an explanation?'

'No,' said Mr Montmorency, rising slowly and yet in such a way as to suggest a sudden situation, 'I can't. And may I, as a busy man, be excused if I ask you, gentlemen, if you have any demand to make of me in connection with my business. What kind of house would you desire me to get for you, sir?'

He opened his blank blue eyes on Rupert, who seemed for the second staggered. Then he recovered himself with perfect common sense and answered:

'I am sorry, Mr Montmorency. The fascination of your remarks has unduly delayed us from joining our friend outside. Pray excuse my apparent impertinence.'

'Not at all, sir,' said the house-agent, taking a South American spider idly from his waistcoat pocket and letting it climb up the slope of his desk. 'Not at all, sir. I hope you will favour me again.'

Rupert Grant dashed out of the office in a gust of anger, anxious to face Lieutenant Keith. He was gone. The dull, starlit street was deserted.

'What do you say now?' cried Rupert to his brother. His brother said nothing now.

We all three strode down the street in silence, Rupert feverish, myself dazed, Basil, to all appearance, merely dull. We walked through grey street after grey street, turning corners, traversing squares, scarcely meeting anyone, except occasional drunken knots of two or three.

In one small street, however, the knots of two or three began abruptly to thicken into knots of five or six and then into great groups and then into a crowd. The crowd was stirring very slightly. But anyone with a knowledge of the eternal populace knows that if the outside rim of a crowd stirs ever so slightly it means that there is madness in the heart and core of the mob. It soon became evident that something really important had happened in the centre of this excitement. We wormed our way to the front, with the cunning which is known only to cockneys, and once there we soon learned the nature of the difficulty. There had been a brawl concerned with some six men, and one of them lay almost dead on the stones of the street. Of the other four, all interesting matters were, as far as we were concerned, swallowed up in one stupendous fact. One of the four survivors of the brutal and perhaps fatal scuffle was the immaculate Lieutenant Keith, his clothes torn to ribbons, his eyes blazing, blood on his knuckles. One other thing, however, pointed at him in a worse manner. A short sword, or very long knife, had been drawn out of his elegant walking stick, and lay in front of him upon the stones. It did not, however, appear to be bloody.

The police had already pushed into the centre with their ponderous omnipotence, and even as they did so, Rupert Grant sprang forward with his incontrollable and intolerable secret.

'That is the man, constable,' he shouted, pointing at the battered lieutenant. 'He is a suspicious character. He did the murder.'

'There's been no murder done, sir,' said the policeman, with his automatic civility. 'The poor man's only hurt. I shall only be able to take the names and addresses of the men in the scuffle and have a good eye kept on them.'

'Have a good eye kept on that one,' said Rupert, pale to the lips, and pointing to the ragged Keith.

'All right, sir,' said the policeman unemotionally, and went the round of the people present, collecting the addresses. When he had completed his task the dusk had fallen and most of the people not immediately connected with the examination had gone away. He still found, however, one eager-faced stranger lingering on the outskirts of the affair. It was Rupert Grant.

'Constable,' he said, 'I have a very particular reason for asking you a question. Would you mind telling me whether that military fellow who dropped his swordstick in the row gave you an address or not?'

'Yes, sir,' said the policeman, after a reflective pause; 'yes, he gave me his address.'

'My name is Rupert Grant,' said that individual, with some pomp. 'I have assisted the police on more than one occasion. I wonder whether you would tell me, as a special favour, what address?'

The constable looked at him.

'Yes,' he said slowly, 'if you like. His address is: The Elms, Buxton Common, near Purley, Surrey.'

'Thank you,' said Rupert, and ran home through the gathering night as fast as his legs could carry him, repeating the address to himself.

Rupert Grant generally came down late in a rather lordly way to breakfast; he contrived, I don't know how, to achieve always the attitude of the indulged younger brother. Next morning, however, when Basil and I came down we found him ready and restless.

'Well,' he said sharply to his brother almost before we sat down to the meal. 'What do you think of your Drummond Keith now?'

'What do I think of him?' enquired Basil slowly. 'I don't think anything of him.'

'I'm glad to hear it,' said Rupert, buttering his toast with an energy that was somewhat exultant. 'I thought you'd come round to my view, but I own I was startled at your not seeing it from the beginning. The man is a translucent liar and knave.'

'I think,' said Basil, in the same heavy monotone as before, 'that I did not make myself clear. When I said that I thought nothing of him I meant grammatically what I said. I meant that I did not think about him; that he did not occupy my mind. You, however, seem to me to think a lot of him, since you think him a knave. I should say he was glaringly good myself.'

'I sometimes think you talk paradox for its own sake,' said Rupert, breaking an egg with unnecessary sharpness. 'What the deuce is the sense of it? Here's a man whose original position was, by our common agreement, dubious. He's a wanderer, a teller of tall tales, a man who doesn't conceal his acquaintance with all the blackest and bloodiest scenes on earth. We take the trouble to follow him to one of his appointments, and if ever two human beings were plotting together and lying to every one else, he and that impossible house-agent were doing it. We followed him home, and the very same night he is in the thick of a fatal, or nearly fatal, brawl, in which he is the only man armed. Really, if this is being glaringly good, I must confess that the glare does not dazzle me.'

Basil was quite unmoved. 'I admit his moral goodness is of a certain kind, a quaint, perhaps a casual kind. He is very fond of change and experiment. But all the points you so ingeniously make against him are mere coincidence or special pleading. It's true he didn't want to talk about his house business in front of us. No man would. It's true that he carries a swordstick. Any man might. It's true he drew it in the shock of a street fight. Any man would. But there's nothing really dubious in all this. There's nothing to confirm – '

As he spoke a knock came at the door.

'If you please, sir,' said the landlady, with an alarmed air, 'there's a policeman wants to see you.'

'Show him in,' said Basil, amid the blank silence.

The heavy, handsome constable who appeared at the door spoke almost as soon as he appeared there.

'I think one of you gentlemen,' he said, curtly but respectfully, 'was present at the affair in Copper Street last night, and drew my attention very strongly to a particular man.'

Rupert half rose from his chair, with eyes like diamonds, but the constable went on calmly, referring to a paper.

'A young man with grey hair. Had light grey clothes, very good, but torn in the struggle. Gave his name as Drummond Keith.'

'This is amusing,' said Basil, laughing. 'I was in the very act of clearing that poor officer's character of rather fanciful aspersions. What about him?'

'Well, sir,' said the constable, 'I took all the men's addresses and had them all watched. It wasn't serious enough to do more than that. All the other addresses are all right. But this man Keith gave a false address. The place doesn't exist.'

The breakfast table was nearly flung over as Rupert sprang up, slapping both his thighs.

'Well, by all that's good,' he cried. 'This is a sign from heaven.'

'It's certainly very extraordinary,' said Basil quietly, with knitted brows. 'It's odd the fellow should have given a false address, considering he was perfectly innocent in the – '

'Oh, you jolly old early Christian duffer,' cried Rupert, in a sort of rapture, 'I don't wonder you couldn't be a judge. You think every one as good as yourself. Isn't the thing plain enough now? A doubtful acquaintance; rowdy stories, a most suspicious conversation, mean streets, a concealed knife, a man nearly killed, and, finally, a false address. That's what we call glaring goodness.'

'It's certainly very extraordinary,' repeated Basil. And he strolled moodily about the room. Then he said: 'You are quite sure, constable, that there's no mistake? You got the address right, and the police have really gone to it and found it was a fraud?'

'It was very simple, sir,' said the policeman, chuckling. 'The place he named was a well-known common quite near London, and our people were down there this morning before any of you were awake. And there's no such house. In fact, there are hardly any houses at all. Though it is so near London, it's a blank moor with hardly five trees on it, to say nothing of Christians. Oh, no, sir, the address was a fraud right enough. He was a clever rascal, and chose one of those scraps of lost England that people know nothing about. Nobody could say offhand that there was not a particular house dropped somewhere about the heath. But as a fact, there isn't.'

Basil's face during this sensible speech had been growing darker and darker with a sort of desperate sagacity. He was cornered almost for the first time since I had known him; and to tell the truth I rather wondered at the almost childish obstinacy which kept him so close to his original prejudice in favour of the wildly questionable lieutenant. At length he said:

'You really searched the common? And the address was really not known in the district – by the way, what was the address?'

The constable selected one of his slips of paper and consulted it, but before he could speak Rupert Grant, who was leaning in the window in a perfect posture of the quiet and triumphant detective, struck in with the sharp and suave voice he loved so much to use.

'Why, I can tell you that, Basil,' he said graciously as he idly plucked leaves from a plant in the window. 'I took the precaution to get this man's address from the constable last night.'

'And what was it?' asked his brother gruffly.

'The constable will correct me if I am wrong,' said Rupert, looking sweetly at the ceiling. 'It was: The Elms, Buxton Common, near Purley, Surrey.'

'Right, sir,' said the policeman, laughing and folding up his papers.

There was a silence, and the blue eyes of Basil looked blindly for a few seconds into the void. Then his head fell back in his chair so suddenly that I started up, thinking him ill. But before I could move further his lips had flown apart (I can use no other phrase) and a peal of gigantic laughter struck and shook the ceiling – laughter that shook the laughter, laughter redoubled, laughter incurable, laughter that could not stop.

Two whole minutes afterwards it was still unended; Basil was ill with laughter; but still he laughed. The rest of us were by this time ill almost with terror.

'Excuse me,' said the insane creature, getting at last to his feet. 'I am awfully sorry. It is horribly rude. And stupid, too. And also unpractical, because we have not much time to lose if we're to get down to that place. The train service is confoundedly bad, as I happen to know. It's quite out of proportion to the comparatively small distance.'

'Get down to that place?' I repeated blankly. 'Get down to what place?'

'I have forgotten its name,' said Basil vaguely, putting his hands in his pockets as he rose. 'Something Common near Purley. Has anyone got a timetable?'

'You don't seriously mean,' cried Rupert, who had been staring in a sort of confusion of emotions. 'You don't mean that you want to go to Buxton Common, do you? You can't mean that!'

'Why shouldn't I go to Buxton Common?' asked Basil, smiling.

'Why should you?' said his brother, catching hold again restlessly of the plant in the window and staring at the speaker.

'To find our friend, the lieutenant, of course,' said Basil Grant. 'I thought you wanted to find him?'

Rupert broke a branch brutally from the plant and flung it impatiently on the floor. 'And in order to find him,' he said, 'you suggest the admirable expedient of going to the only place on the habitable earth where we know he can't be.'

The constable and I could not avoid breaking into a kind of assenting laugh, and Rupert, who had family eloquence, was encouraged to go on with a reiterated gesture:

'He may be in Buckingham Palace; he may be sitting astride the cross of St Paul's; he may be in jail (which I think most likely); he may be in the Great Wheel; he may be in my pantry; he may be in your store cupboard; but out of all the innumerable points of space, there is only one where he has just been systematically looked for and where we know that he is not to be found – and that, if I understand you rightly, is where you want us to go.'

'Exactly,' said Basil calmly, getting into his great-coat; 'I thought you might care to accompany me. If not, of course, make yourselves jolly here till I come back.'

It is our nature always to follow vanishing things and value them if they really show a resolution to depart. We all followed Basil, and I cannot say why, except that he was a vanishing thing, that he vanished decisively with his great-coat and his stick. Rupert ran after him with a considerable flurry of rationality.

'My dear chap,' he cried, 'do you really mean that you see any good in going down to this ridiculous scrub, where there is nothing but beaten tracks and a few twisted trees, simply because it was the first place that came into a rowdy lieutenant's head when he wanted to give a lying reference in a scrape?'

'Yes,' said Basil, taking out his watch, 'and, what's worse, we've lost the train.'

He paused a moment and then added: 'As a matter of fact, I think we may just as well go down later in the day. I have some writing to do, and I think you told me, Rupert, that you thought of going to the Dulwich Gallery. I was rather too impetuous. Very likely he wouldn't be in. But if we get down by the 5.15, which gets to Purley about 6, I expect we shall just catch him.'

'Catch him!' cried his brother, in a kind of final anger. 'I wish we could. Where the deuce shall we catch him now?'

'I keep forgetting the name of the common,' said Basil, as he buttoned up his coat. 'The Elms – what is it? Buxton Common, near Purley. That's where we shall find him.'

'But there is no such place,' groaned Rupert; but he followed his brother downstairs.

We all followed him. We snatched our hats from the hatstand and our sticks from the umbrella stand; and why we followed him we did not and do not know. But we always followed him, whatever was the meaning of the fact, whatever was the nature of his mastery. And the strange thing was that we followed him the more completely the more nonsensical appeared the thing which he said. At bottom, I believe, if he had risen from our breakfast table and said: 'I am going to find the Holy Pig with Ten Tails,' we should have followed him to the end of the world.

I don't know whether this mystical feeling of mine about Basil on this occasion has got any of the dark and cloudy colour, so to speak, of the strange journey that we made the same evening. It was already very dense twilight when we struck southward from Purley. Suburbs and things on the London border may be, in most cases, commonplace and comfortable.

But if ever by any chance they really are empty solitudes they are to the human spirit more desolate and dehumanised than any Yorkshire moors or Highland hills, because the suddenness with which the traveller drops into that silence has something about it as of evil elf-land. It seems to be one of the ragged suburbs of the cosmos half-forgotten by God – such a place was Buxton Common, near Purley.

There was certainly a sort of grey futility in the landscape itself. But it was enormously increased by the sense of grey futility in our expedition. The tracts of grey turf looked useless, the occasional wind-stricken trees looked useless, but we, the human beings, more useless than the hopeless turf or the idle trees. We were maniacs akin to the foolish landscape, for we were come to chase the wild goose that has led men and left men in bogs from the beginning. We were three dazed men under the captaincy of a madman going to look for a man whom we knew was not there in a house that had no existence. A livid sunset seemed to look at us with a sort of sickly smile before it died.

Basil went on in front with his coat collar turned up, looking in the gloom rather like a grotesque Napoleon. We crossed swell after swell of the windy common in increasing darkness and entire silence. Suddenly Basil stopped and turned to us, his hands in his pockets. Through the dusk I could just detect that he wore a broad grin as of comfortable success.

'Well,' he cried, taking his heavily gloved hands out of his pockets and slapping them together, 'here we are at last.'

The wind swirled sadly over the homeless heath; two desolate elms rocked above us in the sky like shapeless clouds of grey. There was not a sign of man or beast to the sullen circle of the horizon, and in the midst of that wilderness Basil Grant stood rubbing his hands with the air of an innkeeper standing at an open door.

'How jolly it is,' he cried, 'to get back to civilisation. That notion that civilisation isn't poetical is a civilised delusion. Wait till you've really lost yourself in nature, among the devilish woodlands and the cruel flowers. Then you'll know that there's no star like the red star of man that he lights on his hearthstone; no river like the red river of man, the good red wine, which you, Mr Rupert Grant, if I have any knowledge of you, will be drinking in two or three minutes in enormous quantities.'

Rupert and I exchanged glances of fear. Basil went on heartily, as the wind died in the dreary trees:

'You'll find our host a much more simple kind of fellow in his own house. I did when I visited him when he lived in the cabin at Yarmouth, and again in the loft at the city warehouse. He's really a very good fellow. But his greatest virtue remains what I said originally.'

'What do you mean?' I asked, finding his speech straying towards a sort of sanity. 'What is his greatest virtue?'

'His greatest virtue,' replied Basil, 'is that he always tells the literal truth.'

'Well, really,' cried Rupert, stamping about between cold and anger, and slapping himself like a cabman, 'he doesn't seem to have been very literal or truthful in this case, nor you either. Why the deuce, may I ask, have you brought us out to this infernal place?'

'He was too truthful, I confess,' said Basil, leaning against the tree; 'too hardly veracious, too severely accurate. He should have indulged in a little more suggestiveness and legitimate romance. But come, it's time we went in. We shall be late for dinner.'

Rupert whispered to me with a white face:

'Is it a hallucination, do you think? Does he really fancy he sees a house?'

'I suppose so,' I said. Then I added aloud, in what was meant to be a cheery and sensible voice, but which sounded in my ears almost as strange as the wind:

'Come, come, Basil, my dear fellow. Where do you want us to go?'

'Why, up here,' cried Basil, and with a bound and a swing he was above our heads, swarming up the grey column of the colossal tree.

'Come up, all of you,' he shouted out of the darkness, with the voice of a schoolboy. 'Come up. You'll be late for dinner.'

The two great elms stood so close together that there was scarcely a yard anywhere, and in some places not more than a foot, between them. Thus occasional branches and even bosses and boles formed a series of footholds that almost amounted to a rude natural ladder. They must, I supposed, have been some sport of growth, Siamese twins of vegetation.

Why we did it I cannot think; perhaps, as I have said, the mystery of the waste and dark had brought out and made primary something wholly mystical in Basil's supremacy. But we only felt that there was a giant's staircase going somewhere, perhaps to the stars; and the victorious voice above called to us out of heaven. We hoisted ourselves up after him.

Half-way up some cold tongue of the night air struck and sobered me suddenly. The hypnotism of the madman above fell from me, and I saw the whole map of our silly actions as clearly as if it were printed. I saw three modern men in black coats who had begun with a perfectly sensible suspicion of a doubtful adventurer and who had ended, God knows how, half-way up a naked tree on a naked moorland, far from that adventurer and all his works, that adventurer who was at that moment, in all probability, laughing at us in some dirty Soho restaurant. He had plenty to laugh at us about, and no doubt he was laughing his loudest; but when I thought what his laughter would be if he knew where we were at that moment, I nearly let go of the tree and fell.

'Swinburne,' said Rupert suddenly, from above, 'what are we doing? Let's get down again,' and by the mere sound of his voice I knew that he too felt the shock of wakening to reality.

'We can't leave poor Basil,' I said. 'Can't you call to him or get hold of him by the leg?'

'He's too far ahead,' answered Rupert; 'he's nearly at the top of the beastly thing. Looking for Lieutenant Keith in the rooks' nests, I suppose.'

We were ourselves by this time far on our frantic vertical journey. The mighty trunks were beginning to sway and shake slightly in the wind. Then I looked down and saw something which made me feel that we were far from the world in a sense and to a degree that I cannot easily describe. I saw that the almost straight lines of the tall elm trees diminished a little in perspective as they fell. I was used to seeing parallel lines taper towards the sky. But to see them taper towards the earth made me feel lost in space, like a falling star.

'Can nothing be done to stop Basil?' I called out.

'No,' answered my fellow climber. 'He's too far up. He must get to the top, and when he finds nothing but wind and leaves he may go sane again. Hark at him above there; you can just hear him talking to himself.'

'Perhaps he's talking to us,' I said.

'No,' said Rupert, 'he'd shout if he was. I've never known him to talk to himself before; I'm afraid he really is bad tonight; it's a known sign of the brain going.'

'Yes,' I said sadly, and listened. Basil's voice certainly was sounding above us, and not by any means in the rich and riotous tones in which he had hailed us before. He was speaking quietly, and laughing every now and then, up there among the leaves and stars.

After a silence mingled with this murmur, Rupert Grant suddenly said, 'My God!' with a violent voice.

'What's the matter – are you hurt?' I cried, alarmed.

'No. Listen to Basil,' said the other in a very strange voice. 'He's not talking to himself.'

'Then he is talking to us,' I cried.

'No,' said Rupert simply, 'he's talking to somebody else.'

Great branches of the elm loaded with leaves swung about us in a sudden burst of wind, but when it died down I could still hear the conversational voice above. I could hear two voices.

Suddenly from aloft came Basil's boisterous hailing voice as before: 'Come up, you fellows. Here's Lieutenant Keith.'

And a second afterwards came the half-American voice we had heard in our chambers more than once. It called out:

'Happy to see you, gentlemen; pray come in.'

Out of a hole in an enormous dark egg-shaped thing, pendent in the branches like a wasps' nest, was protruding the pale face and fierce moustache of the lieutenant, his teeth shining with that slightly Southern air that belonged to him.

Somehow or other, stunned and speechless, we lifted ourselves heavily into the opening. We fell into the full glow of a lamplit, cushioned, tiny room, with a circular wall lined with books, a circular table, and a circular seat around it. At this table sat three people. One was Basil, who, in the instant after alighting there, had fallen into an attitude of marmoreal ease as if he had been there from boyhood; he was smoking a cigar with a slow pleasure. The second was Lieutenant Drummond Keith, who looked happy also, but feverish and doubtful compared with his granite guest. The third was the little bald-headed house-agent with the wild whiskers, who called himself Montmorency. The spears, the green umbrella, and the cavalry sword hung in parallels on the wall. The sealed jar of strange wine was on the mantelpiece, the enormous rifle in the corner.

In the middle of the table was a magnum of champagne. Glasses were already set for us.

The wind of the night roared far below us, like an ocean at the foot of a lighthouse. The room stirred slightly, as a cabin might in a mild sea.

Our glasses were filled, and we still sat there dazed and dumb. Then Basil spoke.

'You seem still a little doubtful, Rupert. Surely there is no further question about the cold veracity of our injured host.'

'I don't quite grasp it all,' said Rupert, blinking still in the sudden glare. 'Lieutenant Keith said his address was – '

'It's really quite right, sir,' said Keith, with an open smile. 'The bobby asked me where I lived. And I said, quite truthfully, that I lived in the elms on Buxton Common, near Purley. So I do. This gentleman, Mr Montmorency, whom I think you have met before, is an agent for houses of this kind. He has a special line in arboreal villas. It's being kept rather quiet at present, because the people who want these houses don't want them to get too common. But it's just the sort of thing a fellow like myself, racketing about in all sorts of queer corners of London, naturally knocks up against.'

'Are you really an agent for arboreal villas?' asked Rupert eagerly, recovering his ease with the romance of reality.

Mr Montmorency, in his embarrassment, fingered one of his pockets and nervously pulled out a snake, which crawled about the table.

'W-well, yes, sir,' he said. 'The fact was – er – my people wanted me very much to go into the house-agency business. But I never cared myself for anything but natural history and botany and things like that. My poor parents have been dead some years now, but – naturally I like to respect their wishes. And I thought somehow that an arboreal villa agency was a sort of – of compromise between being a botanist and being a house-agent.'

Rupert could not help laughing. 'Do you have much custom?' he asked.

'N-not much,' replied Mr Montmorency, and then he glanced at Keith, who was (I am convinced) his only client. 'But what there is – very select.'

'My dear friends,' said Basil, puffing his cigar, 'always remember two facts. The first is that though when you are guessing about anyone who is sane, the sanest thing is the most likely; when you are guessing about anyone who is, like our host, insane, the maddest thing is the most likely. The second is to remember that very plain literal fact always seems fantastic. If Keith had taken a little brick box of a house in Clapham with nothing but railings in front of it and had written "The Elms" over it, you wouldn't have thought there was anything fantastic about that. Simply because it was a great blaring, swaggering lie you would have believed it.'

'Drink your wine, gentlemen,' said Keith, laughing, 'for this confounded wind will upset it.'

We drank, and as we did so, although the hanging house, by a cunning mechanism, swung only slightly, we knew that the great head of the elm tree swayed in the sky like a stricken thistle.

5

The Noticeable Conduct of Professor Chadd

Basil Grant had comparatively few friends besides myself; yet he was the reverse of an unsociable man. He would talk to anyone anywhere, and talk not only well but with perfectly genuine concern and enthusiasm for that person's affairs. He went through the world, as it were, as if he were always on the top of an omnibus or waiting for a train. Most of these chance acquaintances, of course, vanished into darkness out of his life. A few here and there got hooked on to him, so to speak, and became his lifelong intimates, but there was an accidental look about all of them as if they were windfalls, samples taken at random, goods fallen from a goods train or presents fished out of a bran-pie. One would be, let us say, a veterinary surgeon with the appearance of a jockey; another, a mild prebendary with a white beard and vague views; another, a young captain in the Lancers, seemingly exactly like other captains in the Lancers; another, a small dentist from Fulham, in all reasonable certainty precisely like every other dentist from Fulham. Major Brown, small, dry and dapper, was one of these; Basil had made his acquaintance over a discussion in a hotel cloakroom about the right hat, a discussion which reduced the little major almost to a kind of masculine hysterics, the compound of the selfishness of an old bachelor and the scrupulosity of an old maid. They had gone home in a cab together and then dined with each other twice a week until they died. I myself was another. I had met Grant while he was still a judge, on the balcony of the National Liberal Club, and exchanged a few words about the weather. Then we had talked for about an hour about politics and God; for men always talk about the most important things to total strangers. It is because in the total stranger we perceive man himself; the image of God is not disguised by resemblances to an uncle or doubts of the wisdom of a moustache.

One of the most interesting of Basil's motley group of acquaintances was Professor Chadd. He was known to the ethnological world (which is a very interesting world, but a long way off this one) as the second greatest, if not the greatest, authority on the relations of savages to language. He was known to the neighbourhood of Hart Street, Bloomsbury, as a bearded man with a bald head, spectacles, and a patient face, the face of an unaccountable Nonconformist who had forgotten how to be angry. He went to and fro between the British Museum and a selection of blameless teashops, with an armful of books and a poor but honest umbrella. He was never seen without the books and the umbrella, and was supposed (by the lighter wits of the Persian MS room) to go to bed with them in his little brick villa in the neighbourhood of Shepherd's Bush. There he lived with three sisters, ladies of solid goodness, but sinister demeanour. His life was happy, as are almost all the lives of methodical students, but one would not have called it exhilarating. His only hours of exhilaration occurred when his friend, Basil Grant, came into the house, late at night, a tornado of conversation.

Basil, though close on sixty, had moods of boisterous baby-ishness, and these seemed for some reason or other to descend upon him particularly in the house of his studious and almost dingy friend. I can remember vividly (for I was acquainted with both parties and often dined with them) the gaiety of Grant on that particular evening when the strange calamity fell upon the professor. Professor Chadd was, like most of his particular class and type (the class that is at once academic and middle-class), a Radical of a solemn and old-fashioned type. Grant was a Radical himself, but he was that more discriminating and not uncommon type of Radical who passes most of his time in abusing the Radical party. Chadd had just contributed to a magazine an article called 'Zulu Interests and the New Makango Frontier', in which a precise scientific report of his study of the customs of the people of T'Chaka was reinforced by a severe protest against certain interferences with these customs both by the British and the Germans. He was sitting with the magazine in front of him, the lamplight shining on his spectacles, a wrinkle in his forehead, not of anger, but of perplexity, as Basil Grant strode up and down the room, shaking it with his voice, with his high spirits and his heavy tread.

'It's not your opinions that I object to, my esteemed Chadd,' he was saying, 'it's you. You are quite right to champion the Zulus, but for all that you do not sympathise with them. No doubt you know the Zulu way of cooking tomatoes and the Zulu prayer before blowing one's nose; but for all that you don't understand them as well as I do, who don't know an assegai from an alligator. You are more learned, Chadd, but I am more Zulu. Why is it that the jolly old barbarians of this earth are always championed by people who are their antithesis? Why is it? You are sagacious, you are benevolent, you are well informed, but, Chadd, you are not savage. Live no longer under that rosy illusion. Look in the glass. Ask your sisters. Consult the librarian of the British Museum. Look at this umbrella.' And he held up that sad but still respectable article. 'Look at it. For ten mortal years to my certain knowledge you have carried that object under your arm, and I have no sort of doubt that you carried it at the age of eight months, and it never occurred to you to give one wild yell and hurl it like a javelin – thus – '

And he sent the umbrella whizzing past the professor's bald head, so that it knocked over a pile of books with a crash and left a vase rocking.

Professor Chadd appeared totally unmoved, with his face still lifted to the lamp and the wrinkle cut in his forehead.

'Your mental processes,' he said, 'always go a little too fast. And they are stated without method. There is no kind of inconsistency' – and no words can convey the time he took to get to the end of the word – 'between valuing the right of the aborigines to adhere to their stage in the evolutionary process, so long as they find it congenial and requisite to do so. There is, I say, no inconsistency between this concession which I have just described to you and the view that the evolutionary stage in question is, nevertheless, so far as we can form any estimate of values in the variety of cosmic processes, definable in some degree as an inferior evolutionary stage.'

Nothing but his lips had moved as he spoke, and his glasses still shone like two pallid moons.

Grant was shaking with laughter as he watched him.

'True,' he said, 'there is no inconsistency, my son of the red spear. But there is a great deal of incompatibility of temper. I am very far from being certain that the Zulu is on an inferior evolutionary stage, whatever the blazes that may mean. I do not think there is anything stupid or ignorant about howling at the moon or being afraid of devils in the dark. It seems to me perfectly philosophical. Why should a man be thought a sort of idiot because he feels the mystery and peril of existence itself? Suppose, my dear Chadd, suppose it is we who are the idiots because we are not afraid of devils in the dark?'

Professor Chadd slit open a page of the magazine with a bone paper-knife and the intent reverence of the bibliophile.

'Beyond all question,' he said, 'it is a tenable hypothesis. I allude to the hypothesis which I understand you to entertain, that our civilisation is not or may not be an advance upon, and indeed (if I apprehend you), is or may be a retrogression from states identical with or analogous to the state of the Zulus.

Moreover, I shall be inclined to concede that such a proposition is of the nature, in some degree at least, of a primary proposition, and cannot adequately be argued, in the same sense, I mean, that the primary proposition of pessimism, or the primary proposition of the non-existence of matter, cannot adequately be argued. But I do not conceive you to be under the impression that you have demonstrated anything more concerning this proposition than that it is tenable, which, after all, amounts to little more than the statement that it is not a contradiction in terms.'

Basil threw a book at his head and took out a cigar.

'You don't understand,' he said, 'but, on the other hand, as a compensation, you don't mind smoking. Why you don't object to that disgustingly barbaric rite I can't think. I can only say that I began it when I began to be a Zulu, about the age of ten. What I maintained was that although you knew more about Zulus in the sense that you are a scientist, I know more about them in the sense that I am a savage. For instance, your theory of the origin of language, something about its having come from the formulated secret language of some individual creature, though you knocked me silly with facts and scholarship in its favour, still does not convince me, because I have a feeling that that is not the way that things happen. If you ask me why I think so I can only answer that I am a Zulu; and if you ask me (as you most certainly will) what is my definition of a Zulu, I can answer that also. He is one who has climbed a Sussex apple tree at seven and been afraid of a ghost in an English lane.'

'Your process of thought – ' began the immovable Chadd, but his speech was interrupted. His sister, with that masculinity which always in such families concentrates in sisters, flung open the door with a rigid arm and said:

'James, Mr Bingham of the British Museum wants to see you again.'

The philosopher rose with a dazed look, which always indicates in such men the fact that they regard philosophy as a familiar thing, but practical life as a weird and unnerving vision, and walked dubiously out of the room.

'I hope you do not mind my being aware of it, Miss Chadd,' said Basil Grant, 'but I hear that the British Museum has recognised one of the men who have deserved well of their commonwealth. It is true, is it not, that Professor Chadd is likely to be made keeper of Asiatic manuscripts?'

The grim face of the spinster betrayed a great deal of pleasure and a great deal of pathos also. 'I believe it's true,' she said. 'If it is, it will not only be great glory that women, I assure you, feel a great deal, but great relief, which they feel more; relief from worry from a lot of things. James's health has never been good, and while we are as poor as we are he had to do journalism and coaching, in addition to his own dreadful grinding notions and discoveries, which he loves more than man, woman or child. I have often been afraid that unless something of this kind occurred we should really have to be careful of his brain. But I believe it is practically settled.'

'I am delighted,' began Basil, but with a worried face, 'but these red-tape negotiations are so terribly chancy that I really can't advise you to build on hope, only to be hurled down into bitterness. I've known men, and good men like your brother, come nearer than this and be disappointed. Of course, if it is true – '

'If it is true,' said the woman fiercely, 'it means that people who have never lived may make an attempt at living.'

Even as she spoke the professor came into the room still with the dazed look in his eyes.

'Is it true?' asked Basil, with burning eyes.

'Not a bit true,' answered Chadd after a moment's bewilderment. 'Your argument was in three points fallacious.'

'What do you mean?' demanded Grant.

'Well,' said the professor slowly, 'in saying that you could possess a knowledge of the essence of Zulu life distinct from – '

'Oh! confound Zulu life,' cried Grant, with a burst of laughter. 'I mean, have you got the post?'

'You mean the post of keeper of the Asiatic manuscripts,' he said, opening his eye with childlike wonder. 'Oh, yes, I got that. But the real objection to your argument, which has only, I admit, occurred to me since I have been out of the room, is that it does not merely presuppose a Zulu truth apart from the facts, but infers that the discovery of it is absolutely impeded by the facts.'

'I am crushed,' said Basil, and sat down to laugh, while the professor's sister retired to her room, possibly, possibly not.

It was extremely late when we left the Chadds, and it is an extremely long and tiresome journey from Shepherd's Bush to Lambeth. This may be our excuse for the fact that we (for I was stopping the night with Grant) got down to breakfast next day at a time inexpressibly criminal, a time, in point of fact, close upon noon. Even to that belated meal we came in a very lounging and leisurely fashion. Grant, in particular, seemed so dreamy at table that he scarcely saw the pile of letters by his plate, and I doubt if he would have opened any of them if there had not lain on the top that one thing which has succeeded amid modern carelessness in being really urgent and coercive – a telegram. This he opened with the same heavy distraction with which he broke his egg and drank his tea. When he read it he did not stir a hair or say a word, but something, I know not what, made me feel that the motionless figure had been pulled together suddenly as strings are tightened on a slack guitar. Though he said nothing and did not move, I knew that he had been for an instant cleared and sharpened with a shock of cold water. It was scarcely any surprise to me when a man who had drifted sullenly to his seat and fallen into it, kicked it away like a cur from under him and came round to me in two strides.

'What do you make of that?' he said, and flattened out the wire in front of me.

It ran: 'Please come at once. James's mental state dangerous. Chadd.'

'What does the woman mean?' I said after a pause, irritably. 'Those women have been saying that the poor old professor was mad ever since he was born.'

'You are mistaken,' said Grant composedly. 'It is true that all sensible women think all studious men mad. It is true, for the matter of that, all women of any kind think all men of any kind mad. But they don't put it in telegrams, any more than they wire to you that grass is green or God all-merciful. These things are truisms, and often private ones at that. If Miss Chadd has written down under the eye of a strange woman in a post office that her brother is off his head you may be perfectly certain that she did it because it was a matter of life and death, and she can think of no other way of forcing us to come promptly.'

'It will force us of course,' I said, smiling.

'Oh, yes,' he replied; 'there is a cab-rank near.'

Basil scarcely said a word as we drove across Westminster Bridge, through Trafalgar Square, along Piccadilly, and up the Uxbridge Road. Only as he was opening the gate he spoke.

'I think you will take my word for it, my friend,' he said; 'this is one of the most queer and complicated and astounding incidents that ever happened in London or, for that matter, in any high civilisation.'

'I confess with the greatest sympathy and reverence that I don't quite see it,' I said. 'Is it so very extraordinary or complicated that a dreamy somnambulant old invalid who has always walked on the borders of the inconceivable should go mad under the shock of great joy? Is it so very extraordinary that a man with a head like a turnip and a soul like a spider's web should not find his strength equal to a confounding change of fortunes? Is it, in short, so very extraordinary that James Chadd should lose his wits from excitement?'

'It would not be extraordinary in the least,' answered Basil, with placidity. 'It would not be extraordinary in the least,' he repeated, 'if the professor had gone mad. That was not the extraordinary circumstance to which I referred.'

'What,' I asked, stamping my foot, 'was the extraordinary thing?'

'The extraordinary thing,' said Basil, ringing the bell, 'is that he has not gone mad from excitement.'

The tall and angular figure of the eldest Miss Chadd blocked the doorway as the door opened. Two other Miss Chadds seemed in the same way to be blocking the narrow passage and the little parlour. There was a general sense of their keeping something from view. They seemed like three black-clad ladies in some strange play of Maeterlinck,[17] veiling the catastrophe from the audience in the manner of the Greek chorus.

'Sit down, won't you?' said one of them, in a voice that was somewhat rigid with pain. 'I think you had better be told first what has happened.'

Then, with her bleak face looking unmeaningly out of the window, she continued, in an even and mechanical voice:

'I had better state everything that occurred just as it occurred. This morning I was clearing away the breakfast things, my sisters were both somewhat unwell, and had not come down. My brother had just gone out of the room, I believe, to fetch a book. He came back again, however, without it, and stood for some time staring at the empty grate. I said, "Were you looking for anything I could get?" He did not answer, but this constantly happens, as he is often very abstracted. I repeated my question, and still he did not answer. Sometimes he is so wrapped up in his studies that nothing but a touch on the shoulder would make him aware of one's presence, so I came round the table towards him. I really do not know how to describe the sensation which I then had. It seems simply silly, but at the moment it seemed something enormous, upsetting one's brain. The fact is, James was standing on one leg.'

Grant smiled slowly and rubbed his hands with a kind of care.

'Standing on one leg?' I repeated.

'Yes,' replied the dead voice of the woman without an inflection to suggest that she felt the fantasticality of her statement. 'He was standing on the left leg and the right drawn up at a sharp angle, the toe pointing downwards. I asked him if his leg hurt him. His only answer was to shoot the leg straight at right angles to the other, as if pointing to the other with his toe to the wall. He was still looking quite gravely at the fireplace.

'"James, what is the matter?" I cried, for I was thoroughly frightened. James gave three kicks in the air with the right leg, flung up the other, gave three kicks in the air with it also and spun round like a teetotum the other way. "Are you mad?" I cried. "Why don't you answer me?" He had come to a standstill facing me, and was looking at me as he always does, with his lifted eyebrows and great spectacled eyes. When I had spoken he remained a second or two motionless, and then his only reply was to lift his left foot slowly from the floor and describe circles with it in the air. I rushed to the door and shouted for Christina. I will not dwell on the dreadful hours that followed. All three of us talked to him, implored him to speak to us with appeals that might have brought back the dead, but he has done nothing but hop and dance and kick with a solemn silent face. It looks as if his legs belonged to someone else or were possessed by devils. He has never spoken to us from that time to this.'

'Where is he now?' I said, getting up in some agitation. 'We ought not to leave him alone.'

'Doctor Colman is with him,' said Miss Chadd calmly. 'They are in the garden. Doctor Colman thought the air would do him good. And he can scarcely go into the street.'

Basil and I walked rapidly to the window which looked out on the garden. It was a small and somewhat smug suburban garden; the flower beds a little too neat and like the pattern of a coloured carpet; but on this shining and opulent summer day even they had the exuberance of something natural, I had almost said tropical. In the middle of a bright and verdant but painfully circular lawn stood two figures. One of them was a small, sharp-looking man with black whiskers and a very polished hat (I presume Dr Colman), who was talking very quietly and clearly, yet with a nervous twitch, as it were, in his face. The other was our old friend, listening with his old forbearing expression and owlish eyes, the strong sunlight gleaming on his glasses as the lamplight had gleamed the night before, when the boisterous Basil had rallied him on his studious decorum. But for one thing the figure of this morning might have been the identical figure of last night. That one thing was that while the face listened reposefully the legs were industriously dancing like the legs of a marionette. The neat flowers and the sunny glitter of the garden lent an indescribable sharpness and incredibility to the prodigy – the prodigy of the head of a hermit and the legs of a harlequin. For miracles should always happen in broad daylight. The night makes them credible and therefore commonplace.

The second sister had by this time entered the room and came somewhat drearily to the window.

'You know, Adelaide,' she said, 'that Mr Bingham from the Museum is coming again at three.'

'I know,' said Adelaide Chadd bitterly. 'I suppose we shall have to tell him about this. I thought that no good fortune would ever come easily to us.'

Grant suddenly turned round. 'What do you mean?' he said. 'What will you have to tell Mr Bingham?'

'You know what I shall have to tell him,' said the professor's sister, almost fiercely. 'I don't know that we need give it its wretched name. Do you think that the keeper of Asiatic manuscripts will be allowed to go on like that?' And she pointed for an instant at the figure in the garden, the shining, listening face and the unresting feet.

Basil Grant took out his watch with an abrupt movement. 'When did you say the British Museum man was coming?' he said.

'Three o'clock,' said Miss Chadd briefly.

'Then I have an hour before me,' said Grant, and without another word threw up the window and jumped out into the garden. He did not walk straight up to the doctor and lunatic, but strolling round the garden path drew near them cautiously and yet apparently carelessly. He stood a couple of feet off them, seemingly counting halfpence out of his trousers pocket, but, as I could see, looking up steadily under the broad brim of his hat.

Suddenly he stepped up to Professor Chadd's elbow, and said, in a loud familiar voice, 'Well, my boy, do you still think the Zulus our inferiors?'

The doctor knitted his brows and looked anxious, seeming to be about to speak. The professor turned his bald and placid head towards Grant in a friendly manner, but made no answer, idly flinging his left leg about.

'Have you converted Dr Colman to your views?' Basil continued, still in the same loud and lucid tone.

Chadd only shuffled his feet and kicked a little with the other leg, his expression still benevolent and enquiring. The doctor cut in rather sharply. 'Shall we go inside, professor?' he said. 'Now you have shown me the garden. A beautiful garden.

A most beautiful garden. Let us go in,' and he tried to draw the kicking ethnologist by the elbow, at the same time whispering to Grant: 'I must ask you not to trouble him with questions. Most risky. He must be soothed.'

Basil answered in the same tone, with great coolness:

'Of course your directions must be followed out, doctor. I will endeavour to do so, but I hope it will not be inconsistent with them if you will leave me alone with my poor friend in this garden for an hour. I want to watch him. I assure you, Dr Colman, that I shall say very little to him, and that little shall be as soothing as – as syrup.'

The doctor wiped his eyeglass thoughtfully.

'It is rather dangerous for him,' he said, 'to be long in the strong sun without his hat. With his bald head, too.'

'That is soon settled,' said Basil composedly, and took off his own big hat and clapped it on the egglike skull of the professor. The latter did not turn round but danced away with his eyes on the horizon.

The doctor put on his glasses again, looked severely at the two for some seconds, with his head on one side like a bird's, and then saying, shortly, 'All right,' strutted away into the house, where the three Misses Chadd were all looking out from the parlour window on to the garden. They looked out on it with hungry eyes for a full hour without moving, and they saw a sight which was more extraordinary than madness itself.

Basil Grant addressed a few questions to the madman, without succeeding in making him do anything but continue to caper, and when he had done this slowly took a red notebook out of one pocket and a large pencil out of another.

He began hurriedly to scribble notes. When the lunatic skipped away from him he would walk a few yards in pursuit, stop, and make notes again. Thus they followed each other round and round the foolish circle of turf, the one writing in pencil with the face of a man working out a problem, the other leaping and playing like a child.

After about three-quarters of an hour of this imbecile scene, Grant put the pencil in his pocket, but kept the notebook open in his hand, and walking round the mad professor, planted himself directly in front of him.

Then occurred something that even those already used to that wild morning had not anticipated or dreamed. The professor, on finding Basil in front of him, stared with a blank benignity for a few seconds, and then drew up his left leg and hung it bent in the attitude that his sister had described as being the first of all his antics. And the moment he had done it Basil Grant lifted his own leg and held it out rigid before him, confronting Chadd with the flat sole of his boot. The professor dropped his bent leg, and swinging his weight on to it kicked out the other behind, like a man swimming. Basil crossed his feet like a saltire cross, and then flung them apart again, giving a leap into the air. Then before any of the spectators could say a word or even entertain a thought about the matter, both of them were dancing a sort of jig or hornpipe opposite each other; and the sun shone down on two madmen instead of one.

They were so stricken with the deafness and blindness of monomania that they did not see the eldest Miss Chadd come out feverishly into the garden with gestures of entreaty, a gentleman following her. Professor Chadd was in the wildest posture of a *pas de quatre*, Basil Grant seemed about to turn a cartwheel, when they were frozen in their follies by the steely voice of Adelaide Chadd saying, 'Mr Bingham of the British Museum.'

Mr Bingham was a slim, well-clad gentleman with a pointed and slightly effeminate grey beard, unimpeachable gloves, and formal but agreeable manners. He was the type of the over-civilised, as Professor Chadd was of the uncivilised pedant. His formality and agreeableness did him some credit under the

circumstances. He had a vast experience of books and a considerable experience of the more dilettante fashionable salons. But
neither branch of knowledge had accustomed him to the spectacle
of two grey-haired middle-class gentlemen in modern costume
throwing themselves about like acrobats as a substitute for an
after-dinner nap.

The professor continued his antics with perfect placidity, but
Grant stopped abruptly. The doctor had reappeared on the
scene, and his shiny black eyes, under his shiny black hat, moved
restlessly from one of them to the other.

'Dr Colman,' said Basil, turning to him, 'will you entertain
Professor Chadd again for a little while? I am sure that he needs
you. Mr Bingham, might I have the pleasure of a few moments'
private conversation? My name is Grant.'

Mr Bingham, of the British Museum, bowed in a manner that
was respectful but a trifle bewildered.

'Miss Chadd will excuse me,' continued Basil easily, 'if I know
my way about the house.' And he led the dazed librarian rapidly
through the back door into the parlour.

'Mr Bingham,' said Basil, setting a chair for him, 'I imagine
that Miss Chadd has told you of this distressing occurrence.'

'She has, Mr Grant,' said Bingham, looking at the table with
a sort of compassionate nervousness. 'I am more pained than
I can say by this dreadful calamity. It seems quite heart-rending
that the thing should have happened just as we have decided
to give your eminent friend a position which falls far short of
his merits. As it is, of course – really, I don't know what to say.
Professor Chadd may, of course, retain – I sincerely trust he will
– his extraordinarily valuable intellect. But I am afraid – I am
really afraid – that it would not do to have the curator of the
Asiatic manuscripts – er – dancing about.'

'I have a suggestion to make,' said Basil, and sat down
abruptly in his chair, drawing it up to the table.

'I am delighted, of course,' said the gentleman from the British Museum, coughing and drawing up his chair also.

The clock on the mantelpiece ticked for just the moments required for Basil to clear his throat and collect his words, and then he said:

'My proposal is this. I do not know that in the strict use of words you could altogether call it a compromise, still it has something of that character. My proposal is that the Government (acting, as I presume, through your Museum) should pay Professor Chadd £800 a year until he stops dancing.'

'Eight hundred a year!' said Mr Bingham, and for the first time lifted his mild blue eyes to those of his interlocutor – and he raised them with a mild blue stare. 'I think I have not quite understood you. Did I understand you to say that Professor Chadd ought to be employed, in his present state, in the Asiatic manuscript department at eight hundred a year?'

Grant shook his head resolutely.

'No,' he said firmly. 'No. Chadd is a friend of mine, and I would say anything for him I could. But I do not say, I cannot say, that he ought to take on the Asiatic manuscripts. I do not go so far as that. I merely say that until he stops dancing you ought to pay him £800. Surely you have some general fund for the endowment of research.'

Mr Bingham looked bewildered.

'I really don't know,' he said, blinking his eyes, 'what you are talking about. Do you ask us to give this obvious lunatic nearly a thousand a year for life?'

'Not at all,' cried Basil, keenly and triumphantly. 'I never said for life. Not at all.'

'What for, then?' asked the meek Bingham, suppressing an instinct meekly to tear his hair. 'How long is this endowment to run? Not till his death? Till the Judgement Day?'

'No,' said Basil, beaming, 'but just what I said. Till he has stopped dancing.' And he lay back with satisfaction and his hands in his pockets.

Bingham had by this time fastened his eyes keenly on Basil Grant and kept them there.

'Come, Mr Grant,' he said. 'Do I seriously understand you to suggest that the Government pay Professor Chadd an extraordinarily high salary simply on the ground that he has (pardon the phrase) gone mad? That he should be paid more than four good clerks solely on the ground that he is flinging his boots about in the back yard?'

'Precisely,' said Grant composedly.

'That this absurd payment is not only to run on with the absurd dancing, but actually to stop with the absurd dancing?'

'One must stop somewhere,' said Grant. 'Of course.'

Bingham rose and took up his perfect stick and gloves.

'There is really nothing more to be said, Mr Grant,' he said coldly. 'What you are trying to explain to me may be a joke – a slightly unfeeling joke. It may be your sincere view, in which case I ask your pardon for the former suggestion. But, in any case, it appears quite irrelevant to my duties. The mental morbidity, the mental downfall, of Professor Chadd, is a thing so painful to me that I cannot easily endure to speak of it. But it is clear there is a limit to everything. And if the Archangel Gabriel went mad it would sever his connection, I am sorry to say, with the British Museum Library.'

He was stepping towards the door, but Grant's hand, flung out in dramatic warning, arrested him.

'Stop!' said Basil sternly. 'Stop while there is yet time. Do you want to take part in a great work, Mr Bingham? Do you want to help in the glory of Europe – in the glory of science? Do you want to carry your head in the air when it is bald or white because of the part that you bore in a great discovery? Do you want – '

Bingham cut in sharply:

'And if I do want this, Mr Grant – '

'Then,' said Basil lightly, 'your task is easy. Get Chadd £800 a year till he stops dancing.'

With a fierce flap of his swinging gloves Bingham turned impatiently to the door, but in passing out of it found it blocked. Dr Colman was coming in.

'Forgive me, gentlemen,' he said, in a nervous, confidential voice, 'the fact is, Mr Grant, I – er – have made a most disturbing discovery about Mr Chadd.'

Bingham looked at him with grave eyes.

'I was afraid so,' he said. 'Drink, I imagine.'

'Drink!' echoed Colman, as if that were a much milder affair. 'Oh, no, it's not drink.'

Mr Bingham became somewhat agitated, and his voice grew hurried and vague. 'Homicidal mania – ' he began.

'No, no,' said the medical man impatiently.

'Thinks he's made of glass,' said Bingham feverishly, 'or says he's God – or – '

'No,' said Dr Colman sharply; 'the fact is, Mr Grant, my discovery is of a different character. The awful thing about him is – '

'Oh, go on, sir,' cried Bingham, in agony.

'The awful thing about him is,' repeated Colman, with deliberation, 'that he isn't mad.'

'Not mad!'

'There are quite well-known physical tests of lunacy,' said the doctor shortly; 'he hasn't got any of them.'

'But why does he dance?' cried the despairing Bingham. 'Why doesn't he answer us? Why hasn't he spoken to his family?'

'The devil knows,' said Dr Colman coolly. 'I'm paid to judge of lunatics, but not of fools. The man's not mad.'

'What on earth can it mean? Can't we make him listen?' said Mr Bingham. 'Can none get into any kind of communication with him?'

Grant's voice struck in sudden and clear, like a steel bell:

'I shall be very happy,' he said, 'to give him any message you like to send.'

Both men stared at him.

'Give him a message?' they cried simultaneously. 'How will you give him a message?'

Basil smiled in his slow way.

'If you really want to know how I shall give him your message,' he began, but Bingham cried:

'Of course, of course,' with a sort of frenzy.

'Well,' said Basil, 'like this.' And he suddenly sprang a foot into the air, coming down with crashing boots, and then stood on one leg.

His face was stern, though this effect was slightly spoiled by the fact that one of his feet was making wild circles in the air.

'You drive me to it,' he said. 'You drive me to betray my friend. And I will, for his own sake, betray him.'

The sensitive face of Bingham took on an extra expression of distress as of one anticipating some disgraceful disclosure. 'Anything painful, of course – ' he began.

Basil let his loose foot fall on the carpet with a crash that struck them all rigid in their feeble attitudes.

'Idiots!' he cried. 'Have you seen the man? Have you looked at James Chadd going dismally to and fro from his dingy house to your miserable library, with his futile books and his confounded umbrella, and never seen that he has the eyes of a fanatic? Have you never noticed, stuck casually behind his spectacles and above his seedy old collar, the face of a man who might have burned heretics, or died for the philosopher's stone? It is all my fault, in a way: I lit the dynamite of his deadly faith.

I argued against him on the score of his famous theory about language – the theory that language was complete in certain individuals and was picked up by others simply by watching them. I also chaffed him about not understanding things in rough and ready practice. What has this glorious bigot done? He has answered me. He has worked out a system of language of his own (it would take too long to explain); he has made up, I say, a language of his own. And he has sworn that till people understand it, till he can speak to us in this language, he will not speak in any other. And he shall not. I have understood, by taking careful notice; and, by heaven, so shall the others. This shall not be blown upon. He shall finish his experiment. He shall have £800 a year from somewhere till he has stopped dancing. To stop him now is an infamous war on a great idea. It is religious persecution.'

Mr Bingham held out his hand cordially.

'I thank you, Mr Grant,' he said. 'I hope I shall be able to answer for the source of the £800 and I fancy that I shall. Will you come in my cab?'

'No, thank you very much, Mr Bingham,' said Grant heartily. 'I think I will go and have a chat with the professor in the garden.'

The conversation between Chadd and Grant appeared to be personal and friendly. They were still dancing when I left.

6

The Eccentric Seclusion of the Old Lady

The conversation of Rupert Grant had two great elements of interest – first, the long fantasias of detective deduction in which he was engaged, and, second, his genuine romantic interest in the life of London. His brother Basil said of him: 'His reasoning is particularly cold and clear, and invariably leads him wrong. But his poetry comes in abruptly and leads him right.' Whether this was true of Rupert as a whole, or no, it was certainly curiously supported by one story about him which I think worth telling.

We were walking along a lonely terrace in Brompton together. The street was full of that bright blue twilight which comes about half-past eight in summer, and which seems for the moment to be not so much a coming of darkness as the turning on of a new azure illuminator, as if the earth were lit suddenly by a sapphire sun. In the cool blue the lemon tint of the lamps had already begun to flame, and as Rupert and I passed them, Rupert talking excitedly, one after another the pale sparks sprang out of the dusk. Rupert was talking excitedly because he was trying to prove to me the nine hundred and ninety-ninth of his amateur detective theories. He would go about London, with this mad logic in his brain, seeing a conspiracy in a cab accident, and a special providence in a falling fusee. His suspicions at the moment were fixed upon an unhappy milkman who walked in front of us. So arresting were the incidents that afterwards overtook us that I am really afraid that I have forgotten what were the main outlines of the milkman's crime. I think it had something to do with the fact that he had only one small can of milk to carry, and that of that he had left the lid loose and walked so quickly that he spilled milk on the pavement. This showed that he was not thinking of his small burden, and this again showed that he anticipated some other than lacteal business at the end of his walk, and this (taken in conjunction with something about muddy boots) showed something else that I have entirely forgotten. I am afraid that I derided this detailed revelation unmercifully; and I am afraid that Rupert Grant, who, though the best of fellows, had a good deal of the sensitiveness of the artistic temperament, slightly resented my derision. He endeavoured to take a whiff of his cigar, with the placidity which he associated with his profession, but the cigar, I think, was nearly bitten through.

'My dear fellow,' he said acidly, 'I'll bet you half a crown that wherever that milkman comes to a real stop I'll find out something curious.'

'My resources are equal to that risk,' I said, laughing. 'Done.'

We walked on for about a quarter of an hour in silence in the trail of the mysterious milkman. He walked quicker and quicker, and we had some ado to keep up with him; and every now and then he left a splash of milk, silver in the lamplight. Suddenly, almost before we could note it, he disappeared down the area steps of a house. I believe Rupert really believed that the milkman was a fairy; for a second he seemed to accept him as having vanished. Then calling something to me which somehow took no hold on my mind, he darted after the mystic milkman, and disappeared himself into the area.

I waited for at least five minutes, leaning against a lamppost in the lonely street. Then the milkman came swinging up the steps without his can and hurried off clattering down the road. Two or three minutes more elapsed, and then Rupert came bounding up also, his face pale but yet laughing; a not uncommon contradiction in him, denoting excitement.

'My friend,' he said, rubbing his hands, 'so much for all your scepticism. So much for your philistine ignorance of the possibilities of a romantic city. Two and sixpence, my boy, is the form in which your prosaic good nature will have to express itself.'

'What?' I said incredulously, 'do you mean to say that you really did find anything the matter with the poor milkman?'

His face fell.

'Oh, the milkman,' he said, with a miserable affectation at having misunderstood me. 'No, I – I didn't exactly bring anything home to the milkman himself, I – '

'What did the milkman say and do?' I said, with inexorable sternness.

'Well, to tell the truth,' said Rupert, shifting restlessly from one foot to another, 'the milkman himself, as far as merely physical appearances went, just said, "Milk, Miss," and handed in the can. That is not to say, of course, that he did not make some secret sign or some – '

I broke into a violent laugh. 'You idiot,' I said, 'why don't you own yourself wrong and have done with it? Why should he have made a secret sign any more than anyone else? You own he said nothing and did nothing worth mentioning. You own that, don't you?'

His face grew grave.

'Well, since you ask me, I must admit that I do. It is possible that the milkman did not betray himself. It is even possible that I was wrong about him.'

'Then come along with you,' I said, with a certain amicable anger, 'and remember that you owe me half a crown.'

'As to that, I differ from you,' said Rupert coolly. 'The milkman's remarks may have been quite innocent. Even the milkman may have been. But I do not owe you half a crown. For the terms of the bet were, I think, as follows, as I pro-pounded them, that wherever that milkman came to a real stop I should find out something curious.'

'Well?' I said.

'Well,' he answered, 'I jolly well have. You just come with me,' and before I could speak he had turned tail once more and whisked through the blue dark into the moat or basement of the house. I followed almost before I made any decision.

When we got down into the area I felt indescribably foolish – literally, as the saying is, in a hole. There was nothing but a closed door, shuttered windows, the steps down which we had come, the ridiculous well in which I found myself, and the ridiculous man who had brought me there, and who stood there with dancing eyes. I was just about to turn back when Rupert caught me by the elbow.

'Just listen to that,' he said, and keeping my coat gripped in his right hand, he rapped with the knuckles of his left on the shutters of the basement window. His air was so definite that I paused and even inclined my head for a moment towards it. From inside was coming the murmur of an unmistakable human voice.

'Have you been talking to somebody inside?' I asked suddenly, turning to Rupert.

'No, I haven't,' he replied, with a grim smile, 'but I should very much like to. Do you know what somebody is saying in there?'

'No, of course not,' I replied.

'Then I recommend you to listen,' said Rupert sharply.

In the dead silence of the aristocratic street at evening, I stood a moment and listened. From behind the wooden partition, in which there was a long lean crack, was coming a continuous and moaning sound which took the form of the words: 'When shall I get out? When shall I get out? Will they ever let me out?' or words to that effect.

'Do you know anything about this?' I said, turning upon Rupert very abruptly.

'Perhaps you think I am the criminal,' he said sardonically, 'instead of being in some small sense the detective. I came into this area two or three minutes ago, having told you that I knew there was something funny going on, and this woman behind the shutters (for it evidently is a woman) was moaning like mad. No, my dear friend, beyond that I do not know anything about her. She is not, startling as it may seem, my disinherited daughter, or a member of my secret seraglio. But when I hear a human being wailing that she can't get out, and talking to herself like a mad woman and beating on the shutters with her fists, as she was doing two or three minutes ago, I think it worth mentioning, that is all.'

'My dear fellow,' I said, 'I apologise; this is no time for arguing. What is to be done?'

Rupert Grant had a long clasp-knife naked and brilliant in his hand.

'First of all,' he said, 'house-breaking.' And he forced the blade into the crevice of the wood and broke away a huge splinter, leaving a gap and glimpse of the dark window-pane inside. The room within was entirely unlighted, so that for the first few seconds the window seemed a dead and opaque surface, as dark as a strip of slate. Then came a realisation that, though in a sense gradual, made us step back and catch our breath. Two large dim human eyes were so close to us that the window itself seemed suddenly to be a mask. A pale human face was pressed against the glass within, and with increased distinctness, with the increase of the opening came the words:

'When shall I get out?'

'What can all this be?' I said.

Rupert made no answer, but lifting his walking stick and pointing the ferrule like a fencing sword at the glass, punched a hole in it, smaller and more accurate than I should have supposed possible. The moment he had done so the voice spouted out of the hole, so to speak, piercing and querulous and clear, making the same demand for liberty.

'Can't you get out, madam?' I said, drawing near the hole in some perturbation.

'Get out? Of course I can't,' moaned the unknown female bitterly. 'They won't let me. I told them I would be let out. I told them I'd call the police. But it's no good. Nobody knows, nobody comes. They could keep me as long as they liked only – '

I was in the very act of breaking the window finally with my stick, incensed with this very sinister mystery, when Rupert held my arm hard, held it with a curious, still, and secret rigidity as if he desired to stop me, but did not desire to be observed to do so. I paused a moment, and in the act swung slightly round, so that I was facing the supporting wall of the front door steps. The act froze me into a sudden stillness like that of Rupert, for a figure almost as motionless as the pillars of the portico, but unmistakably human, had put his head out from between the doorposts and was gazing down into the area. One of the lighted lamps of the street was just behind his head, throwing it into abrupt darkness. Consequently, nothing whatever could be seen of his face beyond one fact, that he was unquestionably staring at us. I must say I thought Rupert's calmness magnificent. He rang the area bell quite idly, and went on talking to me with the easy end of a conversation which had never had any beginning. The black glaring figure in the portico did not stir. I almost thought it was really a statue. In another moment the grey area was golden with gaslight as the basement door was opened suddenly and a small and decorous housemaid stood in it.

'Pray excuse me,' said Rupert, in a voice which he contrived to make somehow or other at once affable and underbred, 'but we thought perhaps that you might do something for the Waifs and Strays. We don't expect – '

'Not here,' said the small servant, with the incomparable severity of the menial of the non-philanthropic, and slammed the door in our faces.

'Very sad, very sad – the indifference of these people,' said the philanthropist with gravity, as we went together up the steps. As we did so the motionless figure in the portico suddenly disappeared.

'Well, what do you make of that?' asked Rupert, slapping his gloves together when we got into the street.

I do not mind admitting that I was seriously upset. Under such conditions I had but one thought.

'Don't you think,' I said a trifle timidly, 'that we had better tell your brother?'

'Oh, if you like,' said Rupert, in a lordly way. 'He is quite near, as I promised to meet him at Gloucester Road Station. Shall we take a cab? Perhaps, as you say, it might amuse him.'

Gloucester Road Station had, as if by accident, a somewhat deserted look. After a little looking about we discovered Basil Grant with his great head and his great white hat blocking the ticket-office window. I thought at first that he was taking a ticket for somewhere and being an astonishingly long time about it. As a matter of fact, he was discussing religion with the booking-office clerk, and had almost got his head through the hole in his excitement. When we dragged him away it was some time before he would talk of anything but the growth of an oriental fatalism in modern thought, which had been well typified by some of the official's ingenious but perverse fallacies. At last we managed to get him to understand that we had made an astounding discovery. When he did listen, he listened attentively, walking between us up and down the lamplit street, while we told him in a rather feverish duet of the great house in South Kensington, of the equivocal milkman, of the lady imprisoned in the basement, and the man staring from the porch. At length he said:

'If you're thinking of going back to look the thing up, you must be careful what you do. It's no good you two going there. To go twice on the same pretext would look dubious. To go on a different pretext would look worse. You may be quite certain that the inquisitive gentleman who looked at you looked thoroughly, and will wear, so to speak, your portraits next to his heart. If you want to find out if there is anything in this without a police raid I fancy you had better wait outside. I'll go in and see them.'

His slow and reflective walk brought us at length within sight of the house. It stood up ponderous and purple against the last pallor of twilight. It looked like an ogre's castle. And so apparently it was.

'Do you think it's safe, Basil,' said his brother, pausing, a little pale, under the lamp, 'to go into that place alone? Of course we shall be near enough to hear if you yell, but these devils might do something – something sudden – or odd. I can't feel it's safe.'

'I know of nothing that is safe,' said Basil composedly, 'except, possibly – death,' and he went up the steps and rang at the bell. When the massive respectable door opened for an instant, cutting a square of gaslight in the gathering dark, and then closed with a bang, burying our friend inside, we could not repress a shudder. It had been like the heavy gaping and closing of the dim lips of some evil leviathan. A freshening night breeze began to blow up the street, and we turned up the collars of our coats. At the end of twenty minutes, in which we had scarcely moved or spoken, we were as cold as icebergs, but more, I think, from apprehension than the atmosphere. Suddenly Rupert made an abrupt movement towards the house.

'I can't stand this,' he began, but almost as he spoke sprang back into the shadow, for the panel of gold was again cut out of the black house front, and the burly figure of Basil was silhouetted against it coming out. He was roaring with laughter and talking so loudly that you could have heard every syllable across the street. Another voice, or, possibly, two voices, were laughing and talking back at him from within.

'No, no, no,' Basil was calling out, with a sort of hilarious hostility. 'That's quite wrong. That's the most ghastly heresy of all. It's the soul, my dear chap, the soul that's the arbiter of cosmic forces. When you see a cosmic force you don't like, trick it, my boy. But I must really be off.'

'Come and pitch into us again,' came the laughing voice from out of the house. 'We still have some bones unbroken.'

'Thanks very much, I will – goodnight,' shouted Grant, who had by this time reached the street.

'Goodnight,' came the friendly call in reply, before the door closed.

'Basil,' said Rupert Grant, in a hoarse whisper, 'what are we to do?'

The elder brother looked thoughtfully from one of us to the other.

'What is to be done, Basil?' I repeated in uncontrollable excitement.

'I'm not sure,' said Basil doubtfully. 'What do you say to getting some dinner somewhere and going to the Court Theatre tonight? I tried to get those fellows to come, but they couldn't.'

We stared blankly.

'Go to the Court Theatre?' repeated Rupert. 'What would be the good of that?'

'Good? What do you mean?' answered Basil, staring also. 'Have you turned Puritan or Passive Resister, or something? For fun, of course.'

'But, great God in Heaven! What are we going to do, I mean!' cried Rupert. 'What about the poor woman locked up in that house? Shall I go for the police?'

Basil's face cleared with immediate comprehension, and he laughed.

'Oh, that,' he said. 'I'd forgotten that. That's all right. Some mistake, possibly. Or some quite trifling private affair. But I'm sorry those fellows couldn't come with us. Shall we take one of these green omnibuses? There is a restaurant in Sloane Square.'

'I sometimes think you play the fool to frighten us,' I said irritably. 'How can we leave that woman locked up? How can it be a mere private affair? How can crime and kidnapping and murder, for all I know, be private affairs? If you found a corpse in a man's drawing room, would you think it bad taste to talk about it just as if it was a confounded dado or an infernal etching?'

Basil laughed heartily.

'That's very forcible,' he said. 'As a matter of fact, though, I know it's all right in this case. And there comes the green omnibus.'

'How do you know it's all right in this case?' persisted his brother angrily.

'My dear chap, the thing's obvious,' answered Basil, holding a return ticket between his teeth while he fumbled in his waistcoat pocket. 'Those two fellows never committed a crime in their lives. They're not the kind. Have either of you chaps got a halfpenny? I want to get a paper before the omnibus comes.'

'Oh, curse the paper!' cried Rupert, in a fury. 'Do you mean to tell me, Basil Grant, that you are going to leave a fellow creature in pitch darkness in a private dungeon, because you've had ten minutes' talk with the keepers of it and thought them rather good men?'

'Good men do commit crimes sometimes,' said Basil, taking the ticket out of his mouth. 'But this kind of good man doesn't commit that kind of crime. Well, shall we get on this omnibus?'

The great green vehicle was indeed plunging and lumbering along the dim wide street towards us. Basil had stepped from the curb, and for an instant it was touch and go whether we should all have leaped on to it and been borne away to the restaurant and the theatre.

'Basil,' I said, taking him firmly by the shoulder, 'I simply won't leave this street and this house.'

'Nor will I,' said Rupert, glaring at it and biting his fingers. 'There's some black work going on there. If I left it I should never sleep again.'

Basil Grant looked at us both seriously.

'Of course if you feel like that,' he said, 'we'll investigate further. You'll find it's all right, though. They're only two young Oxford fellows. Extremely nice, too, though rather infected with this pseudo-Darwinian business. Ethics of evolution and all that.'

'I think,' said Rupert darkly, ringing the bell, 'that we shall enlighten you further about their ethics.'

'And may I ask,' said Basil gloomily, 'what it is that you propose to do?'

'I propose, first of all,' said Rupert, 'to get into this house; secondly, to have a look at these nice young Oxford men; thirdly, to knock them down, bind them, gag them, and search the house.'

Basil stared indignantly for a few minutes. Then he was shaken for an instant with one of his sudden laughs.

'Poor little boys,' he said. 'But it almost serves them right for holding such silly views, after all,' and he quaked again with amusement, 'there's something confoundedly Darwinian about it.'

'I suppose you mean to help us?' said Rupert.

'Oh, yes, I'll be in it,' answered Basil, 'if it's only to prevent your doing the poor chaps any harm.'

He was standing in the rear of our little procession, looking indifferent and sometimes even sulky, but somehow the instant the door opened he stepped first into the hall, glowing with urbanity.

'So sorry to haunt you like this,' he said. 'I met two friends outside who very much want to know you. May I bring them in?'

'Delighted, of course,' said a young voice, the unmistakable voice of the Isis, and I realised that the door had been opened, not by the decorous little servant girl, but by one of our hosts in person. He was a short, but shapely young gentleman, with curly dark hair and a square, snub-nosed face. He wore slippers and a sort of blazer of some incredible college purple.

'This way,' he said; 'mind the steps by the staircase. This house is more crooked and old-fashioned than you would think from its snobbish exterior. There are quite a lot of odd corners in the place really.'

'That,' said Rupert, with a savage smile, 'I can quite believe.'

We were by this time in the study or back parlour, used by the young inhabitants as a sitting room, an apartment littered with magazines and books ranging from Dante to detective stories. The other youth, who stood with his back to the fire smoking a corncob, was big and burly, with dead brown hair brushed forward and a Norfolk jacket. He was that particular type of man whose every feature and action is heavy and clumsy, and yet who is, you would say, rather exceptionally a gentleman.

'Any more arguments?' he said, when introductions had been effected. 'I must say, Mr Grant, you were rather severe upon eminent men of science such as we. I've half a mind to chuck my D.Sc. and turn minor poet.'

'Bosh,' answered Grant. 'I never said a word against eminent men of science. What I complain of is a vague popular philosophy which supposes itself to be scientific when it is really nothing but a sort of new religion and an uncommonly nasty one. When people talked about the fall of man they knew they were talking about a mystery, a thing they didn't understand. Now that they talk about the survival of the fittest they think they do understand it, whereas they have not merely no notion, they have an elaborately false notion of what the words mean. The Darwinian movement has made no difference to mankind, except that, instead of talking unphilosophically about philosophy, they now talk unscientifically about science.'

'That is all very well,' said the big young man, whose name appeared to be Burrows. 'Of course, in a sense, science, like mathematics or the violin, can only be perfectly understood by specialists. Still, the rudiments may be of public use. Greenwood here,' indicating the little man in the blazer, 'doesn't know one note of music from another. Still, he knows something. He knows enough to take off his hat when they play "God save the King". He doesn't take it off by mistake when they play "Oh, dem Golden Slippers". Just in the same way science – '

Here Mr Burrows stopped abruptly. He was interrupted by an argument uncommon in philosophical controversy and perhaps not wholly legitimate. Rupert Grant had bounded on him from behind, flung an arm round his throat, and bent the giant backwards.

'Knock the other fellow down, Swinburne,' he called out, and before I knew where I was I was locked in a grapple with the man in the purple blazer. He was a wiry fighter, who bent and sprang like a whalebone, but I was heavier and had taken him utterly by surprise. I twitched one of his feet from under him; he swung for a moment on the single foot, and then we fell with a crash amid the litter of newspapers, myself on top.

My attention for a moment released by victory, I could hear Basil's voice finishing some long sentence of which I had not heard the beginning.

'... wholly, I must confess, unintelligible to me, my dear sir, and I need not say unpleasant. Still one must side with one's old friends against the most fascinating new ones. Permit me, therefore, in tying you up in this antimacassar, to make it as commodious as handcuffs can reasonably be while...'

I had staggered to my feet. The gigantic Burrows was toiling in the garotte of Rupert, while Basil was striving to master his mighty hands. Rupert and Basil were both particularly strong, but so was Mr Burrows; how strong, we knew a second afterwards. His head was held back by Rupert's arm, but a convulsive heave went over his whole frame. An instant after his head plunged forward like a bull's, and Rupert Grant was slung head over heels, a catherine wheel of legs, on the floor in front of him. Simultaneously the bull's head butted Basil in the chest, bringing him also to the ground with a crash, and the monster, with a Berserker roar, leaped at me and knocked me into the corner of the room, smashing the waste-paper basket. The bewildered Greenwood sprang furiously to his feet. Basil did the same. But they had the best of it now.

Greenwood dashed to the bell and pulled it violently, sending peals through the great house. Before I could get panting to my feet, and before Rupert, who had been literally stunned for a few moments, could even lift his head from the floor, two footmen were in the room. Defeated even when we were in a majority, we were now outnumbered. Greenwood and one of the footmen flung themselves upon me, crushing me back into the corner upon the wreck of the paper basket. The other two flew at Basil, and pinned him against the wall. Rupert lifted himself on his elbow, but he was still dazed.

In the strained silence of our helplessness I heard the voice of Basil come with a loud incongruous cheerfulness.

'Now this,' he said, 'is what I call enjoying oneself.'

I caught a glimpse of his face, flushed and forced against the bookcase, from between the swaying limbs of my captors and his. To my astonishment his eyes were really brilliant with pleasure, like those of a child heated by a favourite game.

I made several apoplectic efforts to rise, but the servant was on top of me so heavily that Greenwood could afford to leave me to him. He turned quickly to come to reinforce the two who were mastering Basil. The latter's head was already sinking lower and lower, like a leaking ship, as his enemies pressed him down. He flung up one hand just as I thought him falling and hung on to a huge tome in the bookcase, a volume, I afterwards discovered, of St Chrysostom's[18] theology. Just as Greenwood bounded across the room towards the group, Basil plucked the ponderous tome bodily out of the shelf, swung it, and sent it spinning through the air, so that it struck Greenwood flat in the face and knocked him over like a rolling ninepin. At the same instant Basil's stiffness broke, and he sank, his enemies closing over him.

Rupert's head was clear, but his body shaken; he was hanging as best he could on to the half-prostrate Greenwood. They were rolling over each other on the floor, both somewhat enfeebled by their falls, but Rupert certainly the more so. I was still successfully held down. The floor was a sea of torn and trampled papers and magazines, like an immense waste-paper basket. Burrows and his companion were almost up to the knees in them, as in a drift of dead leaves. And Greenwood had his leg stuck right through a sheet of the *Pall Mall Gazette*, which clung to it ludicrously, like some fantastic trouser frill.

Basil, shut from me in a human prison, a prison of powerful bodies, might be dead for all I knew. I fancied, however, that the broad back of Mr Burrows, which was turned towards me, had a certain bend of effort in it as if my friend still needed some holding down. Suddenly that broad back swayed hither and thither. It was swaying on one leg; Basil, somehow, had hold of the other. Burrows' huge fists and those of the footman were battering Basil's sunken head like an anvil, but nothing could get the giant's ankle out of his sudden and savage grip. While his own head was forced slowly down in darkness and great pain, the right leg of his captor was being forced in the air. Burrows swung to and fro with a purple face. Then suddenly the floor and the walls and the ceiling shook together, as the colossus fell, all his length seeming to fill the floor. Basil sprang up with dancing eyes, and with three blows like battering rams knocked the footman into a cocked hat. Then he sprang on top of Burrows, with one antimacassar in his hand and another in his teeth, and bound him hand and foot almost before he knew clearly that his head had struck the floor. Then Basil sprang at Greenwood, whom Rupert was struggling to hold down, and between them they secured him easily. The man who had hold of me let go and turned to his rescue, but I leaped up like a spring released, and, to my infinite satisfaction, knocked the fellow down. The other footman, bleeding at the mouth and quite demoralised, was stumbling out of the room. My late captor, without a word, slunk after him, seeing that the battle was won. Rupert was sitting astride the pinioned Mr Greenwood, Basil astride the pinioned Mr Burrows.

To my surprise the latter gentleman, lying bound on his back, spoke in a perfectly calm voice to the man who sat on top of him.

'And now, gentlemen,' he said, 'since you have got your own way, perhaps you wouldn't mind telling us what the deuce all this is?'

'This,' said Basil, with a radiant face, looking down at his captive, 'this is what we call the survival of the fittest.'

Rupert, who had been steadily collecting himself throughout the latter phases of the fight, was intellectually altogether himself again at the end of it. Springing up from the prostrate Greenwood, and knotting a handkerchief round his left hand, which was bleeding from a blow, he sang out quite coolly:

'Basil, will you mount guard over the captive of your bow and spear and antimacassar? Swinburne and I will clear out the prison downstairs.'

'All right,' said Basil, rising also and seating himself in a leisured way in an armchair. 'Don't hurry for us,' he said, glancing round at the litter of the room, 'we have all the illustrated papers.'

Rupert lurched thoughtfully out of the room, and I followed him even more slowly; in fact, I lingered long enough to hear, as I passed through the room, the passages and the kitchen stairs, Basil's voice continuing conversationally:

'And now, Mr Burrows,' he said, settling himself sociably in the chair, 'there's no reason why we shouldn't go on with that amusing argument. I'm sorry that you have to express yourself lying on your back on the floor, and, as I told you before, I've no more notion why you are there than the man in the moon. A conversationalist like yourself, however, can scarcely be seriously handicapped by any bodily posture. You were saying, if I remember right, when this incidental fracas occurred, that the rudiments of science might with advantage be made public.'

'Precisely,' said the large man on the floor in an easy tone. 'I hold that nothing more than a rough sketch of the universe as seen by science can be...'

And here the voices died away as we descended into the basement. I noticed that Mr Greenwood did not join in the amicable controversy. Strange as it may appear, I think he looked back upon our proceedings with a slight degree of resentment. Mr Burrows, however, was all philosophy and chattiness. We left them, as I say, together, and sank deeper and deeper into the underworld of that mysterious house, which, perhaps, appeared to us somewhat more Tartarean[19] than it really was, owing to our knowledge of its semi-criminal mystery and of the human secret locked below.

The basement floor had several doors, as is usual in such a house; doors that would naturally lead to the kitchen, the scullery, the pantry, the servants' hall, and so on. Rupert flung open all the doors with indescribable rapidity. Four out of the five opened on entirely empty apartments. The fifth was locked. Rupert broke the door in like a bandbox, and we fell into the sudden blackness of the sealed, unlighted room.

Rupert stood on the threshold, and called out like a man calling into an abyss:

'Whoever you are, come out. You are free. The people who held you captive are captives themselves. We heard you crying and we came to deliver you. We have bound your enemies upstairs hand and foot. You are free.'

For some seconds after he had spoken into the darkness there was a dead silence in it. Then there came a kind of muttering and moaning. We might easily have taken it for the wind or rats if we had not happened to have heard it before. It was unmistakably the voice of the imprisoned woman, drearily demanding liberty, just as we had heard her demand it.

'Has anybody got a match?' said Rupert grimly. 'I fancy we have come pretty near the end of this business.'

I struck a match and held it up. It revealed a large, bare, yellow-papered apartment with a dark-clad figure at the other end of it near the window. An instant after it burned my fingers and dropped, leaving darkness. It had, however, revealed something more practical – an iron gas bracket just above my head. I struck another match and lit the gas. And we found ourselves suddenly and seriously in the presence of the captive.

At a sort of workbox in the window of this subterranean breakfast room sat an elderly lady with a singularly high colour and almost startling silver hair. She had, as if designedly to relieve these effects, a pair of Mephistophelian black eyebrows and a very neat black dress. The glare of the gas lit up her piquant hair and face perfectly against the brown background of the shutters. The background was blue and not brown in one place; at the place where Rupert's knife had torn a great opening in the wood about an hour before.

'Madam,' said he, advancing with a gesture of the hat, 'permit me to have the pleasure of announcing to you that you are free. Your complaints happened to strike our ears as we passed down the street, and we have therefore ventured to come to your rescue.'

The old lady with the red face and the black eyebrows looked at us for a moment with something of the apoplectic stare of a parrot. Then she said, with a sudden gust or breathing of relief:

'Rescue? Where is Mr Greenwood? Where is Mr Burrows? Did you say you had rescued me?'

'Yes, madam,' said Rupert, with a beaming condescension. 'We have very satisfactorily dealt with Mr Greenwood and Mr Burrows. We have settled affairs with them very satisfactorily.'

The old lady rose from her chair and came very quickly towards us.

'What did you say to them? How did you persuade them?' she cried.

'We persuaded them, my dear madam,' said Rupert, laughing, 'by knocking them down and tying them up. But what is the matter?'

To the surprise of every one the old lady walked slowly back to her seat by the window.

'Do I understand,' she said, with the air of a person about to begin knitting, 'that you have knocked down Mr Burrows and tied him up?'

'We have,' said Rupert proudly; 'we have resisted their oppression and conquered it.'

'Oh, thanks,' answered the old lady, and sat down by the window.

A considerable pause followed.

'The road is quite clear for you, madam,' said Rupert pleasantly.

The old lady rose, cocking her black eyebrows and her silver crest at us for an instant.

'But what about Greenwood and Burrows?' she said. 'What did I understand you to say had become of them?'

'They are lying on the floor upstairs,' said Rupert, chuckling. 'Tied hand and foot.'

'Well, that settles it,' said the old lady, coming with a kind of bang into her seat again, 'I must stop where I am.'

Rupert looked bewildered.

'Stop where you are?' he said. 'Why should you stop any longer where you are? What power can force you now to stop in this miserable cell?'

'The question rather is,' said the old lady, with composure, 'what power can force me to go anywhere else?'

We both stared wildly at her and she stared tranquilly at us both.

At last I said, 'Do you really mean to say that we are to leave you here?'

'I suppose you don't intend to tie me up,' she said, 'and carry me off? I certainly shall not go otherwise.'

'But, my dear madam,' cried out Rupert, in a radiant exasperation, 'we heard you with our own ears crying because you could not get out.'

'Eavesdroppers often hear rather misleading things,' replied the captive grimly. 'I suppose I did break down a bit and lose my temper and talk to myself. But I have some sense of honour for all that.'

'Some sense of honour?' repeated Rupert, and the last light of intelligence died out of his face, leaving it the face of an idiot with rolling eyes.

He moved vaguely towards the door and I followed. But I turned yet once more in the toils of my conscience and curiosity. 'Can we do nothing for you, madam?' I said forlornly.

'Why,' said the lady, 'if you are particularly anxious to do me a little favour you might untie the gentlemen upstairs.'

Rupert plunged heavily up the kitchen staircase, shaking it with his vague violence. With mouth open to speak he stumbled to the door of the sitting room and scene of battle.

'Theoretically speaking, that is no doubt true,' Mr Burrows was saying, lying on his back and arguing easily with Basil; 'but we must consider the matter as it appears to our sense. The origin of morality…'

'Basil,' cried Rupert, gasping, 'she won't come out.'

'Who won't come out?' asked Basil, a little cross at being interrupted in an argument.

'The lady downstairs,' replied Rupert. 'The lady who was locked up. She won't come out. And she says that all she wants is for us to let these fellows loose.'

'And a jolly sensible suggestion,' cried Basil, and with a bound he was on top of the prostrate Burrows once more and was unknotting his bonds with hands and teeth.

'A brilliant idea. Swinburne, just undo Mr Greenwood.'

In a dazed and automatic way I released the little gentleman in the purple jacket, who did not seem to regard any of the proceedings as particularly sensible or brilliant. The gigantic Burrows, on the other hand, was heaving with herculean laughter.

'Well,' said Basil, in his cheeriest way, 'I think we must be getting away. We've so much enjoyed our evening. Far too much regard for you to stand on ceremony. If I may so express myself, we've made ourselves at home. Goodnight. Thanks so much. Come along, Rupert.'

'Basil,' said Rupert desperately, 'for God's sake come and see what you can make of the woman downstairs. I can't get the discomfort out of my mind. I admit that things look as if we had made a mistake. But these gentlemen won't mind perhaps...'

'No, no,' cried Burrows, with a sort of Rabelaisian uproariousness. 'No, no, look in the pantry, gentlemen. Examine the coal-hole. Make a tour of the chimneys. There are corpses all over the house, I assure you.'

This adventure of ours was destined to differ in one respect from others which I have narrated. I had been through many wild days with Basil Grant, days for the first half of which the sun and the moon seemed to have gone mad. But it had almost invariably happened that towards the end of the day and its adventure things had cleared themselves like the sky after rain, and a luminous and quiet meaning had gradually dawned upon me. But this day's work was destined to end in confusion worse confounded. Before we left that house, ten minutes afterwards, one half-witted touch was added which rolled all our minds in cloud. If Rupert's head had suddenly fallen off on the floor, if wings had begun to sprout out of Greenwood's shoulders, we could scarcely have been more suddenly stricken. And yet of this we had no explanation. We had to go to bed that night with the prodigy and get up next morning with it and let it stand in our memories for weeks and months. As will be seen, it was not until months afterwards that by another accident and in another way it was explained. For the present I only state what happened.

When all five of us went down the kitchen stairs again, Rupert leading, the two hosts bringing up the rear, we found the door of the prison again closed. Throwing it open we found the place again as black as pitch. The old lady, if she was still there, had turned out the gas: she seemed to have a weird preference for sitting in the dark.

Without another word Rupert lit the gas again. The little old lady turned her birdlike head as we all stumbled forward in the strong gaslight. Then, with a quickness that almost made me jump, she sprang up and swept a sort of old-fashioned curtsey or reverence. I looked quickly at Greenwood and Burrows, to whom it was natural to suppose this subservience had been offered. I felt irritated at what was implied in this subservience, and desired to see the faces of the tyrants as they received it. To my surprise they did not seem to have seen it at all: Burrows was paring his nails with a small penknife. Greenwood was at the back of the group and had hardly entered the room. And then an amazing fact became apparent. It was Basil Grant who stood foremost of the group, the golden gaslight lighting up his strong face and figure. His face wore an expression indescribably conscious, with the suspicion of a very grave smile. His head was slightly bent with a restrained bow. It was he who had acknowledged the lady's obeisance. And it was he, beyond any shadow of reasonable doubt, to whom it had really been directed.

'So I hear,' he said, in a kindly yet somehow formal voice, 'I hear, madam, that my friends have been trying to rescue you. But without success.'

'No one, naturally, knows my faults better than you,' answered the lady with a high colour. 'But you have not found me guilty of treachery.'

'I willingly attest it, madam,' replied Basil, in the same level tones, 'and the fact is that I am so much gratified with your exhibition of loyalty that I permit myself the pleasure of exercising some very large discretionary powers. You would not leave this room at the request of these gentlemen. But you know that you can safely leave it at mine.'

The captive made another reverence. 'I have never complained of your injustice,' she said. 'I need scarcely say what I think of your generosity.'

And before our staring eyes could blink she had passed out of the room, Basil holding the door open for her.

He turned to Greenwood with a relapse into joviality. 'This will be a relief to you,' he said.

'Yes, it will,' replied that immovable young gentleman with a face like a sphinx.

We found ourselves outside in the dark blue night, shaken and dazed as if we had fallen into it from some high tower.

'Basil,' said Rupert at last, in a weak voice, 'I always thought you were my brother. But are you a man? I mean – are you only a man?'

'At present,' replied Basil, 'my mere humanity is proved by one of the most unmistakable symbols – hunger. We are too late for the theatre in Sloane Square. But we are not too late for the restaurant. Here comes the green omnibus!' and he had leaped on it before we could speak.

* * *

As I said, it was months after that Rupert Grant suddenly entered my room, swinging a satchel in his hand and with a general air of having jumped over the garden wall, and implored me to go with him upon the latest and wildest of his expeditions. He proposed to himself no less a thing than the discovery of the actual origin, whereabouts, and headquarters of the source of all our joys and sorrows – the Club of Queer Trades. I should expand this story for ever if I explained how ultimately we ran this strange entity to its lair. The process meant a hundred interesting things. The tracking of a member, the bribing of a cabman, the fighting of roughs, the lifting of a paving stone, the finding of a cellar, the finding of a cellar below the cellar, the finding of the subterranean passage, the finding of the Club of Queer Trades.

I have had many strange experiences in my life, but never a stranger one than that I felt when I came out of those rambling, sightless, and seemingly hopeless passages into the sudden splendour of a sumptuous and hospitable dining room, surrounded upon almost every side by faces that I knew. There was Mr Montmorency, the Arboreal House-Agent, seated between the two brisk young men who were occasionally vicars, and always Professional Detainers. There was Mr P.G. Northover, founder of the Adventure and Romance Agency. There was Professor Chadd, who invented the dancing language.

As we entered, all the members seemed to sink suddenly into their chairs, and with the very action the vacancy of the presidential seat gaped at us like a missing tooth.

'The president's not here,' said Mr P.G. Northover, turning suddenly to Professor Chadd.

'N – no,' said the philosopher, with more than his ordinary vagueness. 'I can't imagine where he is.'

'Good heavens,' said Mr Montmorency, jumping up, 'I really feel a little nervous. I'll go and see.' And he ran out of the room.

An instant after he ran back again, twittering with a timid ecstasy.

'He's there, gentlemen – he's there all right – he's coming in now,' he cried, and sat down. Rupert and I could hardly help feeling the beginnings of a sort of wonder as to who this person might be who was the first member of this insane brotherhood. Who, we thought indistinctly, could be maddest in this world of madmen: what fantastic was it whose shadow filled all these fantastics with so loyal an expectation?

Suddenly we were answered. The door flew open and the room was filled and shaken with a shout, in the midst of which Basil Grant, smiling and in evening dress, took his seat at the head of the table.

How we ate that dinner I have no idea. In the common way I am a person particularly prone to enjoy the long luxuriance of the club dinner. But on this occasion it seemed a hopeless and endless string of courses. Hors d'oeuvre sardines seemed as big as herrings, soup seemed a sort of ocean, larks were ducks, ducks were ostriches until that dinner was over. The cheese course was maddening. I had often heard of the moon being made of green cheese. That night I thought the green cheese was made of the moon. And all the time Basil Grant went on laughing and eating and drinking, and never threw one glance at us to tell us why he was there, the king of these capering idiots.

At last came the moment which I knew must in some way enlighten us, the time of the club speeches and the club toasts. Basil Grant rose to his feet amid a surge of songs and cheers.

'Gentlemen,' he said, 'it is a custom in this society that the president for the year opens the proceedings not by any general toast of sentiment, but by calling upon each member to give a brief account of his trade. We then drink to that calling and to all who follow it. It is my business, as the senior member, to open by stating my claim to membership of this club. Years ago, gentlemen, I was a judge; I did my best in that capacity to do justice and to administer the law. But it gradually dawned on me that in my work, as it was, I was not touching even the fringe of justice. I was seated in the seat of the mighty, I was robed in scarlet and ermine; nevertheless, I held a small and lowly and futile post. I had to go by a mean rule as much as a postman, and my red and gold was worth no more than his. Daily there passed before me taut and passionate problems, the stringency of which I had to pretend to relieve by silly imprisonments or silly damages, while I knew all the time, by the light of my living common sense, that they would have been far better relieved by a kiss or a thrashing, or a few words of explanation, or a duel, or a tour in the West Highlands. Then, as this grew on me, there grew on me continuously the sense of a mountainous frivolity. Every word said in the court, a whisper or an oath, seemed more connected with life than the words I had to say. Then came the time when I publicly blasphemed the whole bosh, was classed as a madman and melted from public life.'

Something in the atmosphere told me that it was not only Rupert and I who were listening with intensity to this statement.

'Well, I discovered that I could be of no real use. I offered myself privately as a purely moral judge to settle purely moral differences. Before very long these unofficial courts of honour (kept strictly secret) had spread over the whole of society. People were tried before me not for the practical trifles for which nobody cares, such as committing a murder, or keeping a dog without a licence. My criminals were tried for the faults which really make social life impossible. They were tried before me for selfishness, or for an impossible vanity, or for scandal-mongering, or for stinginess to guests or dependents. Of course these courts had no sort of real coercive powers. The fulfilment of their punishments rested entirely on the honour of the ladies and gentlemen involved, including the honour of the culprits. But you would be amazed to know how completely our orders were always obeyed. Only lately I had a most pleasing example. A maiden lady in South Kensington whom I had condemned to solitary confinement for being the means of breaking off an engagement through backbiting, absolutely refused to leave her prison, although some well-meaning persons had been inopportune enough to rescue her.'

Rupert Grant was staring at his brother, his mouth fallen agape. So, for the matter of that, I expect, was I. This, then, was the explanation of the old lady's strange discontent and her still stranger content with her lot. She was one of the culprits of his Voluntary Criminal Court. She was one of the clients of his Queer Trade.

We were still dazed when we drank, amid a crash of glasses, the health of Basil's new judiciary. We had only a confused sense of everything having been put right, the sense men will have when they come into the presence of God. We dimly heard Basil say:

'Mr P.G. Northover will now explain the Adventure and Romance Agency.'

And we heard equally dimly Northover beginning the statement he had made long ago to Major Brown. Thus our epic ended where it had begun, like a true cycle.

A Defence of
Detective Stories

In attempting to reach the genuine psychological reason for the popularity of detective stories, it is necessary to rid ourselves of many mere phrases. It is not true, for example, that the populace prefer bad literature to good, and accept detective stories because they are bad literature. The mere absence of artistic subtlety does not make a book popular. Bradshaw's *Railway Guide* contains few gleams of psychological comedy, yet it is not read aloud uproariously on winter evenings. If detective stories are read with more exuberance than railway guides, it is certainly because they are more artistic. Many good books have fortunately been popular; many bad books, still more fortunately, have been unpopular. A good detective story would probably be even more popular than a bad one. The trouble in this matter is that many people do not realise that there is such a thing as a good detective story; it is to them like speaking of a good devil. To write a story about a burglary is, in their eyes, a sort of spiritual manner of committing it. To persons of somewhat weak sensibility this is natural enough; it must be confessed that many detective stories are as full of sensational crime as one of Shakespeare's plays.

There is, however, between a good detective story and a bad detective story as much, or, rather more, difference than there is between a good epic and a bad one. Not only is a detective story a perfectly legitimate form of art, but it has certain definite and real advantages as an agent of the public weal.

The first essential value of the detective story lies in this, that it is the earliest and only form of popular literature in which is expressed some sense of the poetry of modern life. Men lived among mighty mountains and eternal forests for ages before they realised that they were poetical; it may reasonably be inferred that some of our descendants may see the chimney-pots as rich a purple as the mountain peaks, and find the lampposts as old and natural as the trees. Of this realisation of a great city itself as something wild and obvious the detective story is certainly the *Iliad*. No one can have failed to notice that in these stories the hero or the investigator crosses London with something of the loneliness and liberty of a prince in a tale of elfland, that in the course of that incalculable journey the casual omnibus assumes the primal colours of a fairy ship. The lights of the city begin to glow like innumerable goblin eyes, since they are the guardians of some secret, however crude, which the writer knows and the reader does not. Every twist of the road is like a finger pointing to it; every fantastic skyline of chimney-pots seems wildly and derisively signalling the meaning of the mystery.

This realisation of the poetry of London is not a small thing. A city is, properly speaking, more poetic even than a countryside, for while Nature is a chaos of unconscious forces, a city is a chaos of conscious ones. The crest of the flower or the pattern of the lichen may or may not be significant symbols. But there is no stone in the street and no brick in the wall that is not actually a deliberate symbol – a message from some man, as much as if it were a telegram or a postcard. The narrowest street possesses, in every crook and twist of its intention, the soul of the man who built it, perhaps long in his grave. Every brick has as human a hieroglyph as if it were a graven brick of Babylon; every slate on the roof is as educational a document as if it were a slate covered with addition and subtraction sums. Anything which tends, even under the fantastic form of the minutiae of Sherlock Holmes, to assert this romance of detail in civilisation, to emphasise this unfathomably human character in flints and tiles, is a good thing. It is good that the average man should fall into the habit of looking imaginatively at ten men in the street even if it is only on the chance that the eleventh might be a notorious thief. We may dream, perhaps, that it might be possible to have another and higher romance of London, that men's souls have stranger adventures than their bodies, and that it would be harder and more exciting to hunt their virtues than to hunt their crimes. But since our great authors (with the admirable exception of Stevenson) decline to write of that thrilling mood and moment when the eyes of the great city, like the eyes of a cat, begin to flame in the dark, we must give fair credit to the popular literature which, amid a babble of pedantry and preciosity, declines to regard the present as prosaic or the common as commonplace. Popular art in all ages has been interested in contemporary manners and costume; it dressed the groups around the Crucifixion in the garb of Florentine gentlefolk or Flemish burghers. In the last century it was the custom for distinguished actors to present Macbeth in a powdered wig and ruffles. How far we are ourselves in this age from such conviction of the poetry of our own life and manners may easily be conceived by anyone who chooses to imagine a picture of Alfred the Great toasting the cakes dressed in tourist's knickerbockers, or a performance of *Hamlet* in which the Prince appeared in a frock-coat, with a crepe band round his hat. But this instinct of the age to look back, like Lot's wife, could not go on for ever. A rude, popular literature of the romantic possibilities of the modern city was bound to arise. It has arisen in the popular detective stories, as rough and refreshing as the ballads of Robin Hood.

There is, however, another good work that is done by detective stories. While it is the constant tendency of the Old Adam to rebel against so universal and automatic a thing as civilisation, to preach departure and rebellion, the romance of police activity keeps in some sense before the mind the fact that civilisation itself is the most sensational of departures and the most romantic of rebellions. By dealing with the unsleeping sentinels who guard the outposts of society, it tends to remind us that we live in an armed camp, making war with a chaotic world, and that the criminals, the children of chaos, are nothing but the traitors within our gates. When the detective in a police romance stands alone, and somewhat fatuously fearless amid the knives and fists of a thieves' kitchen, it does certainly serve to make us remember that it is the agent of social justice who is the original and poetic figure; while the burglars and footpads are merely placid old cosmic conservatives, happy in the immemorial respectability of apes and wolves. The romance of the police force is thus the whole romance of man. It is based on the fact that morality is the most dark and daring of conspiracies. It reminds us that the whole noiseless and unnoticeable police management by which we are ruled and protected is only a successful knight-errantry.

Notes

1. Gustave Doré (1832–83), French artist, engraver and illustrator.
2. A London club on Pall Mall, founded in 1824.
3. King's Counsel.
4. Victoria Cross.
5. The Battle of Kandahar, which took place on 1st September 1880, was the last major conflict of the second Anglo-Afghan War (1878–80). The British forces were led by General Frederick Roberts (1832–1914).
6. Bedford Park is in Chiswick, London. It is the earliest garden suburb.
7. Horatio Herbert Kitchener, 1st Earl Kitchener (1850–1916), British field marshal, diplomat and statesman.
8. Robert Baden-Powell, 1st Baron Baden-Powell (1857–1941), Lieutenant General in the British army, a writer and the founder of the Scout movement.
9. A religious sect founded in 1846 by the Reverend Henry James Prince (1811–99).
10. A religious sect named after Edward Irving (1792–1834), a deposed Presbyterian minister.
11. Sir Christopher Wren (1632–1723), architect who designed many London churches, including St Paul's Cathedral.
12. Archibald Philip Primrose, 5th Earl of Rosebery (1847–1929), British statesman and Prime Minister from 1894–5.
13. A Roman festival for women only.
14. A woman's bonnet in the shape of a hood, with a projecting rim on the front side to shade the face.
15. Fridtjof Nansen (1861–1930), Norwegian explorer, scientist and diplomat.
16. Mohammed Abdullah Hassan (1864–1920), called 'Mad Mullah' by the British, religious and nationalist leader in Somalia.
17. Maurice Maeterlinck (1862–1949), Belgian poet, playwright and essayist.
18. St John Chrysostom (349–407) was the archbishop of Constantinople.
19. In Greek mythology, Tartarus is an abyss below Hades used as a dungeon of torment and suffering.

Biographical note

Gilbert Keith Chesterton was born in 1874 in Campden Hill in Kensington, London and was educated at St Paul's School. He went on to attend illustration classes at the Slade School of Art and also to study literature at University College London.

Chesterton made his name as a journalist, a job he termed 'the easiest of all professions'. He worked at first as a freelance art and literary critic, and in 1902 was offered a weekly column in the *Daily News*. Later, in 1905, he began a column in *The Illustrated London News*, for which he would write for the next thirty years. He also wrote with Hilaire Belloc at *The Speaker*, a partnership that led Bernard Shaw to coin the term 'Chesterbelloc', and he contributed regularly to the *Eye Witness*, later renamed *New Witness*. In 1925 he founded his own newspaper, *G.K.'s Weekly*, which ran until 1936.

As well as a journalist, Chesterton was a prolific writer of novels, plays and literary criticism. His first novel, *The Napoleon of Notting Hill*, was published in 1904 and in 1912 came the first appearance of Chesterton's famous Father Brown in *The Innocence of Father Brown*. His poetry tended to celebrate Englishness, for example in 'The Rolling English Road' (1914), while his literary criticism included works on Robert Browning (1903) and Bernard Shaw (1910) and a much-admired book on Dickens (1906). He also published many volumes of religious, social and political essays, including *Orthodoxy* (1909) and *The Everlasting Man* (1925). His *Autobiography* appeared in 1936.

Chesterton converted to Catholicism in 1922 and died in 1936 at his home in Beaconsfield, Buckinghamshire, where he is buried in the Catholic cemetery.

HESPERUS PRESS

Hesperus Press, as suggested by the Latin motto, is committed to bringing near what is far – far both in space and time. Works written by the greatest authors, and unjustly neglected or simply little known in the English-speaking world, are made accessible through new translations and a completely fresh editorial approach. Through these classic works, the reader is introduced to the greatest writers from all times and all cultures.

For more information on Hesperus Press, please visit our website:
www.hesperuspress.com

ET REMOTISSIMA PROPE

MODERN VOICES